SMEARED

By

Johnnie E Sanders

Published by Kinetic Digital Publishers

www.kineticdigitalpublishers.com

For permissions, inquiries, or other correspondence, please visit our website

Paperback ISBN: 979-8-90235-062-0

Hardcover ISBN: 979-8-90235-063-7

eBook ISBN: 979-8-90235-061-3

LCCN: 2026903311

BIRMINGHAM IS MY CITY. I'M DEVIN JAMES, THE PUBLIC DEFENDER OF MY CITY. THEREFORE, I AM ALWAYS ON WATCH. THIS IS MY STORY.

SMEARED

Chapter 1
"Bad People Sometimes Behave Like Angels"

Jackson Wallace had the appearance of a 42-year-old polished politician. His father, the judge, had molded him so he seemed perfect. Even so, Jackson Wallace hadn't left his reputation to chance. Better than that, he'd honed it, crafted it, and displayed it so skillfully and naturally that his sincerity captured all:

"...in lower tracks, second-rate schools; to face a future of joblessness or marginal employment. We can't hand down these disadvantages to future generations. Many of us are afraid of change and fight change of any kind. What we ought to be doing is creating change. Change that attacks poverty. Change that provides an economic network that brings jobs to our city..."

Jackson Wallace knew all so well about networking. He'd married for political reasons, and he'd moved up from court reporter to prosecutor to city councilman. His social skills had created a wide network of allies, linked him to the most powerful families and groups in Birmingham, the Battles, the James, the Wrights, the Happy Hour Fund, and the Masonic Order, including the 5,000 people who had shown up to support his announcement speech for mayor of Birmingham.

"...Yes, there will be growing pains, and those stuck in the past who don't want to move forward will eventually become extinct. Those rough edges have to be smoothed off. I'm tired of hearing ridiculous excuses. The companies are coming and jobs with them. If you want a piece of this payday, elevate your minds and get off your behinds and prepare for your future jobs of tomorrow. This is how we attack poverty! A good paycheck is how we maintain a good life! This is my top priority for our city!"

The crowd loved Jackson Wallace, and he fed on their praise, venturing through the crowd, shaking hands, kissing babies, as well as the ladies. The women loved his charm, as well as the fact that Jackson Wallace was a handsome, tall, broad man with a heroic flare to him, and the people believed in him because he had a plan, a vision, and knew where he wanted to take the city.

Jackson Wallace was living out a role of his own creation, a role he'd fantasized about his entire life. As a prosecutor, he was a headliner, going after the big fish, the crime lords the same people he'd grown up with, sat in classrooms with, played pee-wee and high school sports with. Being from Birmingham, Jackson Wallace knew personally who to target to brand himself as the city's watchdog. He directed the investigations and rode shotgun literally.

Part of Jackson Wallace's appeal was his dark side, his ruthless determination that bordered on being vaguely cruel to make sure justice was served, or he just got his way, which went unnoticed and unknown to almost everyone besides Jackson Wallace's lifelong best friend and partner in crime, Pho.

Over the years, Jackson Wallace had cleared the competition while Pho had grown their crime syndicate that was basically adult after-hour spots, consisting of gaming and escorts, in a sophisticated atmosphere with heavily armed security. Even though Jackson Wallace lived for the limelight, no one else knew of his partnership, not even the judge. When Jackson Wallace frequented one of the locations, he was wise enough to play the guest role of Pho but was only seen by a few trusted eyes.

Jackson Wallace was in a cheerful mood, ready to celebrate. Over the years, his joy was derived from knowing he was successfully manipulating the masses. As he looked over the upscale casino-style establishment from behind the tinted window of Pho's office, his blood pumped faster, engorged him, knowing his dreams were coming to full fruition.

"The city will soon be mine!"

"What's gonna become of our businesses?"

"I'm going to fight to legitimize them, but until then, they stay in the shadows."

Jackson Wallace's personal waitress slash escort entered the office. She was an exotic mix of Mexican and Black. Her body was so ripe in her skimpy, revealing uniform that she barely looked legal to pop the bottle of champagne she had. Once she'd filled Jackson Wallace and Pho's flutes, she silently stepped to the side and waited while they toasted.

"To our future."

"To our future." Pho downed his flute and stood eyeing Jackson Wallace, then smiled at the escort. "I'm going to go walk the floor and see who's cheating."

As soon as the door closed behind him, the escort went to her knees while undoing Jackson Wallace's zipper and digging out his primed erection. Her submissive position heightened his excitement, looking down at her as she served him.

Chapter 2
Compassion in The Community

The placement director of the Gate City Development Housing Units seemed to be an odd career choice for my wife, Pearl. Her elegance didn't fit even at 40 with very little makeup and dressed in modest clothing couldn't tone down her beauty, her sophistication, her statue being a maple complected amazon with the thighs, ass, breasts and hips of a goddess she stood out in the poverty-stricken, crime-ridden projects, but her caring, compassionate heart made the position a perfect match for her.

Pearl's office was connected to the recreation center. An elderly woman entered the office with her three young, unruly grandchildren, the youngest close to three years old, the oldest no older than six.

Pearl immediately gave each child a piece of candy from a jar; she kept on her desk just for that purpose. She'd worked for the county for close to 20 years and always with the underprivileged.

The elderly woman didn't give Pearl a chance to speak. "I'm sorry about disturbing you, honey. ... Stop that!" Without any pause, she popped the oldest child's hand who was about to go back into the candy jar. "... Boobe got life. Missy and these damn kids have been staying with me since he was arrested. They took their house and every penny. She's found a job, but. ... I love 'em, but the apartment you got me in is too small for all of us."

The youngest child started crying, backing away from the elderly woman's intense look. The little girl stumbled and fell.

Pearl quickly picked her up, comforting the child on her shoulder, "Mrs. Moore, I can put you on the list for a three-bedroom apartment, or I can put Missy on the list for an apartment." The child had stopped crying, but Pearl was still holding her, pacing with the child. "I've got you. I've got you."

"Put Missy on the list. How long do you think it'll take?"

"I don't know, but I'll see if I can expedite it."

"That means speed it up, right?"

"Yes, me' am."

"Thank you, honey. Thank you... You can put her down. She's got to walk. ...You can put her down. She's got to walk..." Seeing the reluctance of Pearl to release the child, sympathy filled her tone. "You and Devin should try one more time. Thank you again, honey."

It was a difficult time in my wife's life as well as mine. We'd unexpectedly lost our second child less than half a year earlier. Neither one of us had properly grieved.

Once Pearl was alone, she called me. "...Are you going to be home for dinner?"

"Probably, haven't had enough people signed up for the tournament."

"Good. I love you."

"I love you, too."

"I'll see you when you get home."

After the death, we both had become distant, neglecting each other. Our sex life had become less frequent to non-existent. She was such an affectionate person and longed for it. She knew she was sexy, but needed to feel it. Not from the cat calls from the guys in the gym that were made toward her as she headed out, ending her day's work, though they did help her self-esteem. She was a little self-conscious. She was now middle-aged, and to her, her body wasn't as tight as it once was. To me, her body was more voluptuous, sexier than it had ever been.

Pearl stopped by the market. She'd decided to prepare a romantic dinner with my favorite bottle of wine. The Galleria was across the street, and she was drawn to Victoria's Secret.

Candlelight lit the dining room. Smooth mood music played in the background. A romantic dinner for two sat on the table, while Pearl sat in front of it dressed in a sexy silk night gown. Everything seemed perfect except the tears in Pearl's eyes, the empty bottle of wine, and the fact that she sat alone all told the real story of how dissatisfied, disappointed, just plain unhappy she was.

Really, about how we both felt.

Pearl's cell rang, and she knew it was me. "What happened?"

"More people than you can imagine signed up at the last minute. Don't wait up. I don't know how much longer this will be."

Pearl ended the call, and her tears fell. What she couldn't imagine was how the happiest, healthiest relationship had become so rocky.

Chapter 3
Navigating Grief

I'm Devin James; my life was at a crossroad. I was fighting personal issues that haunted me. I was possessed by them. My entire life, I'd been stable and secure, but at that point in my life, all I wanted to do was crawl into my shell and focus all my attention on the memories of my daughters. I had quit practicing law. Mentally, I was too disturbed to represent anyone. Fortunately, I could focus at my children's clothing store, Tiny Tots' Closet. Pearl and I had opened it after the twins were born, so there, the essence of my angels was with me.

Business had slowed with the economy, but the side hobbies I'd started with my mother and Melody, my daughter, who was 17, promoting spades tournaments, dance contests, and small blues concerts had become highly successful. They were for the older crowd, but Melody had been mature beyond her years, which came from hanging out too much with her grandmother. I could concentrate and actually enjoy myself while promoting.

As I cleaned up and locked up the recreation center with my mother and a few of her friends I'd hired to help, it felt as if Melody was beside me, just as exhausted, just as excited about the turnout.

Once I entered my home, I saw the remains of Pearl's attempt at a romantic evening.

Our bedroom was dimly lit by moonlight, but I could see Pearl's figure in bed. I knew she wasn't asleep. She couldn't sleep without me being home.

Once upon a time, she would've been at the spades tournament with me. We would've even entered as partners. But we were handling the death differently.

I was holding on while it seemed Pearl was trying to forget. Pearl snuggled close to me. I needed her warmth, "I've got a new marketing strategy I want to use for the store. I want to tap into the girl's college funds."

Pearl was still at the stage where she was uncomfortable discussing our daughters. "I closed them already. I mentioned it to you about using half to buy CDs..." She rolled over, facing me. Her expression told that she had something serious she wanted to discuss, but knew it was touchy. "...I want to use the other half to buy a new home...."

I couldn't speak. I couldn't believe she could even think of such a thing.

"Since the sales are dropping, we could accept the last offer." People were offering to buy Tiny Tots' Closet all the time, but I wasn't going to sell. We'd opened it for our girls. It was theirs. Pearl was trying to erase my daughters from my life. I felt like I was lying next to a stranger, not the woman I'd loved for 23 years of the 42 years I'd lived.

I got out of bed without saying a word, then went to Ivy, my five-year-old daughter's room. I could hear her crying.

Melody was rocking her, comforting her, "It's all right. Daddy isn't going to allow Mommy to sell the house or the store. Right, Daddy?"

It wasn't my imagination or subconscious. I could see, feel, and hear, and I could talk to my daughters—but to Pearl, who was standing in the doorway, I seemed disturbed, rocking while lying on my daughter's bed. We'd left her room the same for twelve years since her death. It had been too emotionally painful for us to change the room. So I'd cleaned it while Pearl avoided it. She wouldn't dare enter the room, so she backed away.

To keep from going totally insane, I was seeing a therapist to help deal with my grief. My doctor was the youngest of the Wright sisters, Annette. I'd attended high school with two of her older sisters. They shared the same beauty and brains as my doctor. She was the city's psychiatrist, and since I was on leave from my public defender job but still listed as a city employee, the city paid for my sessions.

I'd tried to get Pearl to attend the sessions with me, but she wasn't ready, as she'd put it.

The sessions were useful because they gave me a release, someone to vent to. "If we do, I won't be able to talk to my angels," I felt as if I was fighting to keep my daughters alive.

"They can hear you wherever you are."

"Yes, but their essence is at home and Tiny Tots' Closet." I hadn't told Annette I could actually see them and converse with them. I was afraid she would admit me to the mental ward.

Chapter 4
Teenage Drama

Late February, spring had come early. The high school day had ended. My niece Jasmine and her friend Angel were headed to cheerleader practice. Both girls had mature bodies for being only 17. They looked grown and thought they were, but they were actually Daddy's naïve little ambitious girls.

The baseball team was stretching and warming up for practice.

Jasmine was scanning the field when she spotted Misty, who was also a cheerleader, playfully coming out of the dugout with Monte, Jasmine's supposed boyfriend. He was a corn-fed, muscular country boy, handsome, and came from a good family, plus he was the best friend of A.J., Jasmine's brother.

Once Monte's eyes noticed Jasmine, he instantly started explaining, "I was helping her –"

"I don't care." Jasmine was doing everything in her power to keep a calm demeanor.

"Tell her?" Monte was somewhat begging Misty to speak up, but Misty only smirked and trotted off. "She tricked me into going down there!"

"I said I don't care." Jasmine did, but really didn't. She was like her father; my big brother, focused on bigger things in life. She participated in extracurricular activities: the mathematics team, dancing, the school newspaper, and the cheerleading squad, but each served a purpose. She was politically minded but still a young girl who dreamed of a fairy tale romance.

Later that evening, Jasmine was still pissed, ripping the poster of Monte off her bedroom wall, balling it up, and throwing it into the trash. She then focused on the outfit lying across her bed, before grimacing at Angel, who was dressed and looking out of the window into the darkness.

Angel felt her stare, then turned to see that Jasmine was dressing for bed.

"You know how Misty is."

"I do. And I know what's on Monte's mind, too. I'm not going. But you have a good time."

"You sound like an old woman."

A car pulled up with its headlights off. A.J., my nephew, got out. He was my brother's son by a woman other than Jasmine's mother but he and Jasmine were as close as any brother and sister could be.

A.J. helped Angel out of the window, then peeped back in. "Are you coming?"

"No."

"Why not?"

"I don't want to."

"You're tripping. The only reason Monte's going is that he thought you were coming."

"I'm not, so bye." To finalize her statement, Jasmine turned off the lamp and got under the covers.

Chapter 5
Love and Business

Amere was my older brother. Our lives as children had followed a bumpy, winding road. Our mother had raised us alone, but had taught us to earn our chances. I'd become a private person; we both were, sort of. I held back, only speaking on things I was sure of, while Amere would more often than not came up with ideas that bordered on the fantastic. He wouldn't tell anyone; he would just try to bring them to life. He liked to do things his way, in his own time, in his own inimitable style. No set plan. He would explore all his ideas to see which made money, which worked.

Despite the contrast in personalities, in some ways my brother and I were twins. Our looks stopped people, but our brains captured them. We both understood human nature, the reason for our chosen professions. Amere was a businessman, a genius when it came to making money. Wingouts, unisex salons, a realty company, a shopping plaza, 12 homes, and two sets of 42-unit apartments. He wasn't the richest man in Birmingham, but he was wealthy and appeared healthy. The only sign of any problem was the small bottle of milk of magnesia he carried in his pocket.

People would say my brother was a player or a rolling stone but he didn't play. He was straightforward with everyone, especially both of his households. He was married to Belle, Jasmine's mother, but he'd been dating both Belle and Viola since they were in the eighth grade. Viola was A.J.'s mother. Both of his relationships with the mothers of his children were entirely different, as were Belle and Viola's attitudes. His relationship with Belle was based on their bickering, their form of intimacy, but neither would permanently leave the other. Viola played her role with no complaints, happy with their arrangement. Neither relationship was a master-slave thing.

My brother didn't use his wealth to exert control over them. To both women, he was the very air they breathed. I can honestly say he loved them both, too. Both women were trifectas; face, body, and brains and financially independent.

Amere only had two children, but he treated his pits and his street fighters as if they were his children. He'd bought a ranch along the Warrior River where he trained his dogs and his street fighters. Amere was as tough on his dogs as he was on his street fighters. He took a hands-on approach and wasn't above getting in the pit with either dog or man. He would go toe-to-toe with anyone and used the same mentality in business and at everything else. Amere took risks, but they were calculated.

Besides the love for his family and for making money, Amere's next greatest passion was gambling. He toured the southern cities with his team of pits and street fighters. If there was a big stake or even a chance at a big pot, Amere and his teams were there. The street fighters' matches were just as brutal and bloody as the pit bulls, mountain men battling with every ounce of energy in their bodies. The only rule was to do whatever it took to win.

One of Amere's fighters appeared close to being choked out, but somehow managed to reach back and take hold of the guy's nuts, squeezing and pulling as hard as he could. The fighter released the choke hold and delivered two powerful punches to the back of Amere's fighter's head. But when the fighter tried to re-establish the choke hold, Amere's fighter bit down into the other fighter's forearm; locked on like a pit bull. Blood oozed from his mouth and the fighter's arm. The pain was so severe that all the other fighters could do was give a blood-curdling scream.

Amere's fighter's teeth met, and a hunk of flesh was gone from the other fighter's forearm. Blood squirted from it like a fountain. Two quick elbows to the face stopped the screaming but didn't knock the fighter out. Amere's fighter was just as dazed and tired, but went on the attack. Once he realized his punches didn't have the power to finish the guy, he started biting, along with punching. The screaming immediately started, and the other fighter quickly tapped out.

Chapter 6
Confrontation and Connection

The physicality of my brother and Belle's relationship was ridiculous. Often, words weren't enough to express what Belle was feeling. Through confrontation was how they communicated their affection; fussing and fucking or fighting and fucking. She needed the connection, and over the years, it had become a cycle.

The time was one in the morning when Amere got home. Belle was in bed when he entered the bedroom, headed for the shower.

"You can do that in a little while. Come here. Please."

"I've been fighting dogs all night. I smell like them."

"I don't care."

Amere knew she just wanted him because she thought he'd been over to Viola's. "Let me take a shower first."

Belle sat up and watched him undress. "Why didn't you take a shower before you left the bitch's house?"

Amere's non-reply; he just stared at Belle, infuriating her more than anything he could've said. She quickly got out of bed and tried to block the bathroom entrance.

Amere was 6'3" and normally about 240 pounds, but had slimmed down to 220, while Belle was a nice size for a woman, being 5'11", 165 pounds. But she wasn't a match for my brother. He allowed her to push him, but when she went to slap him, he pushed her aside. She bounced hard off the wall, which dazed her.

"Muthafucka, I'ma get your ass for this!"

He eyed her, made sure she wasn't really hurt, then got into the shower. "I told you I don't feel like playing."

By the time Amere was done with his shower, the police were entering his bedroom. He didn't say how disappointed he was that Belle had involved the police, but his facial expression showed it. "Y'all have wasted your time coming out here. Her crazy ass ain't taking the medication. She's liable to say anything."

"I don't take medication!"

"That's what I said."

"Sir, did you hit her?"

"No!"

"He pushed me into the wall!"

"You pushed me several times. Look, she's PMS'ing. She loves me, but she's pissed over nothing."

"Mr. James, I think it would be best if one of you left the premises until you guys have had time to cool down, or I'll have to arrest you both."

Jasmine stepped to the door, half asleep in her pajamas. Amere saw how one of the male officers did a double-take, focusing on Jasmine's body. "Baby, everything's fine. It's just your mom acting a fool again. Go back to sleep."

Amere got dressed, staring at Belle, whose house robe had come open. "Close your damn robe!"

"You're the one who got asshole naked in front of 'em!"

"Because your retarded ass called them."

The police escorted Amere out of his own home. Belle followed them to the door. The censored lights automatically lit the massive estate. Belle seemed to get angrier as she watched Amere getting into his car, "Take your ass to that flea-bitten hoe. She probably does smell like a dog!"

Amere only honked the horn and threw up the peace sign as he drove off behind the police.

The home Amere had bought for Viola and A.J. was also in Lakewood, and just as big and nice.

A.J. was snoring while his television showed ESPN. Amere turned it off, then went to Viola and his bedroom. The door was shut, but he opened it with no concern. Once he got into bed, Viola didn't say a word or show bitterness. She just snuggled close to him and went back to sleep.

It was morning when Amere was awakened by Viola shaking the bed. His cell was ringing, as was the landline to the house.

Viola was staring at the caller ID. "Call her before I answer my phone and really piss her crazy ass off."

Viola was naturally laidback, but under the wrong circumstances could become just as crazy as Belle. She stepped away and continued getting dressed, allowing Amere his privacy as he answered his cell.

"Call the police, but don't call me." Amere hung up on Belle, then stomach pains doubled him over. As soon as the pains subsided, Amere downed a huge swallow of milk of magnesia, then noticed Viola staring with a concerned look.

"Y'all done gave me ulcers."

"Don't put y'all on it. I'm not sweating you. You're allowing that crazy heifer to stress you out. Your breakfast is ready. You need to talk to A.J., or you're going to be a granddad soon, as much time as he's spending with Angel."

Amere had a full wardrobe there, which was to be expected; it was his home. He entered the kitchen dressed professionally as any Fortune 500 executive. Once Amere sat at the kitchen table, Viola prepped his five-pointed pocket handkerchief.

A.J.'s expression was one of surprise and pride to see his parents interact so affectionately.

"Thank you, babe. Good morning..." Gritting with a nod, while checking out his son's sweater and jeans, showing his approval.

"Good morning...." A.J.'s smirk changed to serious. "...What made you stop this way?"

"I live here..." Then sized up his son and realized it was more to it. "...Speak your mind."

"I don't like you treating mom, like she's your jump off."

"Speak English when you talk to me."

"You're treating my mom like a hoe."

Amere stopped eating and gave A.J. a double take, but controlled his temper.

"You don't buy a hoe a house, and you most definitely don't have a child with a hoe. You pimp a hoe. You get paid off a hoe. I love your mom and your step-mom." My brother's philosophy wasn't about scaring his children straight; he used straight talk, no sugar coating. He didn't hide anything because he was willing to face the consequences of his actions.

"Why, why do you make her cry if you love her so?"

"Your mom doesn't cry over me."

Viola was a strong-willed, independent woman, so the idea of her crying over any man was unbelievable, yet her expression said it was true.

"I've heard her crying herself to sleep many nights when you're not here. What if she had someone else?"

Amere deliberately made eye contact with Viola, "...I would step away. But not from you. You have my blood running through your body. I can't walk away from you even if you hate me. I'm going to always love you..."

Amere knew and understood that A.J. was defending his mother's reputation and honor.

"...Your step-mother and your mom and I have had this understanding since before –"

"Please! Don't... A.J., you're going to be late." Viola knew how complicated their triangle of a relationship was, but at the same time, for most of the time, it was the stabilizer of their relationship.

"Shit, ain't a need to sugar coat it and make him hate me."

"Dad, I don't hate you. I love you, man."

Chapter 7
Dick Envy

Behind Belle's sexiness and street mentality was a formidable mathematical mind. It was uncanny the transformation Belle's personality went through while at work or in public, she was flossy but highly sophisticated and professional. Regardless of how hard Belle tried, she couldn't suppress her suspicion of men, but most of the time she kept it from affecting her work as a bank branch assistant manager. She wasn't as brutally honest at work with employees and customers, but she was honest to the point that they understood whether she was satisfied or dissatisfied. What could've been a hindrance or a great attribute was that she was so extremely efficient that delegating was not an option. She preferred doing things herself so she wouldn't have to worry if it was done right.

Belle hadn't been informed of the meeting that was taking place in the branch manager's office with the regional director, the bank manager, and Eli, who was another assistant branch manager. She felt disrespected. She'd been with the bank for almost two decades. All she could concentrate on was confronting the regional director as soon as he exited the office. She could see them shaking hands with half hugs, being more friendly than usual business shakes. They'd agreed upon something. She could tell.

Her statue alone was enough to stop any man. "Eric, I didn't know you were stopping by."

The regional manager looked a little surprised. "I don't know why not. Floyd knew weeks ago."

Floyd had been the branch manager for six years, but Eli and Belle had run the branch even when Floyd was a schmoozer of an assistant manager. He'd faked it till he'd made it, but in his case, he just kept faking it.

Belle knew Floyd was a true bullshit artist. "Did you pitch the proposal?"

Floyd got tongue-tied while Eric got somewhat excited, "Yes, he did. It's reassuring when a branch manager shows such initiative, ..." She wanted to scream. Floyd had pitched her proposal as his own. But she didn't cause a scene. She understood being faithful to your boss was the key to moving up the ladder, so she listened like a poor deluded drone, "... is such an example for you and Eli, our new branch manager, to feed off."

"An opening became available for a branch manager?"

"Yes. We're opening a branch in Lakewood."

Belle controlled her temper but was furious while only smirking at Floyd. She wasn't angry at Eli; she and he both had become completely obsessed with grabbing that next rung on the ladder. But he'd seemingly calculated his opportunities and moves more precisely.

"Were you interested in becoming a branch manager?"

"I am interested."

"I'll keep that in mind for the next available position."

"Please. Thank you." Belle couldn't understand how she hadn't been thought of for the position of branch manager, but watched as they left the branch for her to run alone. But she did understand that they all had dicks and were probably frat brothers looking out for one another.

Belle hit the gym five days a week. It wasn't only to stay physically fit but mentally stable as well. It was therapeutic for her and Pearl and April, who was thicker than them but only because she was short and hipped, while still just as sexy. They were a support system, had been since their teenage years so they called their workouts vent sessions. My brother, Doc, and I called them bitchfest well, Amere did.

The ladies did light weights, yoga, jogging, and aerobics on rotating evenings. All three ladies had their issues, and at the base of them, a man was the cause.

They were running the indoor tracks, airing their problems, Belle, particularly, was venting and sweating, highly frustrated. "Shit, fuck patience! Eighteen years waiting on Amere to straighten his act up. Sixteen at the branch. How much longer? Now Amere is only fucking me twice a month. I mean, what's the fuck?"

Belle sprinted ahead, not wanting them to realize she was crying instead of sweating.

Chapter 8
Unofficial Mayor

Ellis Collins was the dark horse that had whispers floating around the city that he would or should throw his name in the race for mayor. Everyone respected Ellis Collins, and once you got to know him, you couldn't help but like him, but the wishful thinking was coming mostly from influential groups and people associated with Kappa Alpha Psi who wanted one of our own in control, directing the city.

Ellis Collins was Amere's sands; they'd crossed at UAB together, two years before I did. But Ellis Collin and I were closer; we'd worked somewhat together our entire career. He was a policeman on patrol, catching the allergic criminals while I defended them, and I did my best to prove them innocent. We butted heads a lot, but he was straight-laced while understanding there were areas of grey. His passion wanted their punishment to fit the crime. If it was a first-time offender or excruciating circumstances were present, Ellis Collins would actually speak on behalf of the defendants at their sentencing. He also expressed his concerns for the safety of the community when it came to a habitual offender, requesting a lengthy sentence.

After years of dedicated work on the force, Ellis Collins had become a detective, and our careers became even more embattled. But I understood his views on a safer city.

Pearl and Melisa, Ellis Collins' wife, had been friends forever, and we had them over, or we went over often, making sure our careers didn't end our friendships. Our daughters played with his daughter. Pearl was her godmother. When tragedy had struck, a paroled rapist wanting revenge had killed Melisa, Pearl and I did our best to help Ellis Collins get through it. And when we'd lost Ivy, our first daughter, Ellis Collins had been there for me and helped me to continue defending the public.

Ellis Collins had gone on with life, fighting for his cause while raising his now 10th-grade daughter, Ebony, with the help of his parents and his live-in mother-in-law. He'd turned down two offers to serve as captain of the police department because it would take time away from being with his daughter.

Ellis Collins was no longer going to therapy but was dating Dr. Wright. They made a beautiful couple. Ellis Collins was the handsome, very stylish, heroic type that matched perfectly with Annette's brainy, sensual style. She had accompanied Ellis Collins to one of Jackson Wallace's rallies.

"creating to live in. These are my promises! And I want you to hold me accountable for my promise. .... God bless America and God bless Birmingham. Thank you all for your support."

Annette was focused on Ellis Collins' face, analyzing his nonverbal response. He felt her stare. "Stop it."

Annette was also one of the ones who wished Ellis Collins would enter the mayor's election.

"What do you think?"

"I agree with his viewpoints and his direction." His cell vibrated. It was a text. "Duty calls. Tomorrow night. Right?"

"Sure."

The house was massive and beautiful. Plastic red cups littered the lawn; three police units were in the drive-about near the front entrance. A coroner arrived seconds after Ellis Collins had parked. The inside of the luxurious home was trashed with the remains of a party, a skip party. High school students would pick a house, learn the residents' schedule, then hack the alarm system and literally have a party while the owners were at work.

But this one had gone drastically wrong.

Two teenage girls were crying while being questioned by the police. Another teenage girl was stretched out on the sofa, appeared to be asleep, but the limpness in her body, to the trained eyes of Ellis Collin, knew she was dead. He inspected the body for bruises, but none were visible. She was the same age as Ebony, his daughter. He had to step over vomit when he approached the officer interviewing the other girls.

"... We don't do drugs."

"Were you drinking?"

Both girls focused on Ellis Collins' voice, his parental anger, and then his face.

"Yes, sir. But she had a seizure."

"We called 911. We could've left with everyone else."

A middle-aged businesswoman could be heard screaming at the officer who was trying to block her entrance into the house.

"...I don't have children! Only my husband and I live here." Her answer stunned the officer, and she used the moment to get by but froze in her tracks once seeing the inside of her home. She scanned to the two girls and Ellis Collins. "I want them arrested for breaking and entering, vandalism, and destruction of property! I'm pressing full charges! Put their asses in cuffs!"

"Ma'am, I'm sorry. I'm going to have to ask you to step outside. This is possibly a crime scene."

"Damn right it is, and you have two of the criminals."

The girls were already distraught over the loss of their friend, and Ellis Collins recognized it. He kept a moderate tone with the woman.

"Mrs.–"

"Cunningham."

"Mrs. Cunningham, your home is insured. You will be reimbursed. That young girl lying on your sofa, nothing will give her life back. ..."

The lady hadn't realized the child was dead.

"I want to catch the person or people who contributed to her death and who were behind gathering the people in your home."

Chapter 9
Power Play

Strings were being pulled; back-room meetings were being had. Judge Wallace was tapping into every influential resource he knew, trying to ensure a victory come November, even though it was early March. He'd gathered other judges, business owners, preachers; all leaders in the communities of Birmingham, all key pieces with the ability to reach the people, but most importantly, these leaders mirrored Judge Wallace and Jackson Wallace's ideology to various degrees, and were Shriners as were both Judge Wallace and Jackson Wallace.

The judge had charisma as well as a bully mentality. "The making of a successful leader has always been a joint process, and with direct communication, we'll have this. We'll right our city on the path deemed necessary and sound..."

The meeting had two purposes: One, a show of power to influence others to get on board; and two, to open up negotiations that would later be individually made one-on-one, favors for donations, fundraising events. It was back scratching at its finest.

Chapter 10
Impact

Jackson Wallace was a brilliant politician. He'd designed a plan that would play on the emotional ties to both the rich and the poor. He needed their votes and donations. He'd staged a rally in front of the court building.

"...This law has been in place for two decades. But I'm giving a final warning to all, because starting tomorrow, this law will be enforced ..."

It was more of a message to the rich that their taxpaying dollars wouldn't be spent on anyone not willing to legally contribute to society.

The meeting Jackson Wallace held directly afterward with the housing superintendent and the project directors relayed his sentiments to the poor who needed government housing to survive.

"... I'm asking you to do extra, because as we know a lot of us don't read the newspapers or watch the news. So for their benefit, I'm asking; will you, project directors spread the word to your tenants, this is their last warning."

Ninety percent of the directors were female, and his gesture alone touched them with his show of compassion and understanding. Pearl was among the directors nodding in agreement, sitting next to her supervisor, who also had an appreciative smile on her face.

Instead of impersonal phone calls, Pearl had decided to personally stop by the tenant's project apartments that were listed as possibly selling drugs.

The projects respected her, liked her, so when she was seen walking through the projects, all illegal activities were put aside at least until she'd passed. Pearl spoke with the grandmothers, mothers, baby's mothers, and girlfriends, trying to be as sensitive as possible.

"Mrs. James, ain't nobody selling drugs here, I promise you."

"This applies to anywhere. If anyone is caught selling drugs in this city, and has this apartment listed as their address everyone here gets evicted. ..."

She saw the effects of the message registering on their faces. "... I'm not suggesting anyone is selling drugs, because if I had a notion, I'm supposed to evict you or lose my job. But City Councilman Jackson Wallace has required that everyone be informed and warned because the evictions will be enforced."

That alone was some of the best campaigning Jackson Wallace devised, because it struck deep into the hearts and minds of all who heard it.

Chapter 11
Whispers of Loss

I was hurting, mentally grasping to hold onto my daughters and my sanity. When I was around others, I went through the motions, but once alone, I would openly talk with my angels. Ivy, my youngest, didn't understand and would ask questions that tore at my heart, tested my sanity.

"Daddy, why haven't I grown as big as Melody? Daddy, who's the oldest, me or Melody? But wasn't I born first?"

Both of my daughters were there with me in the storage area of Tiny Tots. I wasn't imagining it. It wasn't my rationale questioning my reality. But they were twins.

Ivy, at five, had caught the West Nile virus from a mosquito bite and never recovered.

"You're with daddy, that's all that matters."

One of my salespersons opened the door. Her eyes told me she'd heard me talking, but she was sensitive to my circumstances. "The crowd is growing. We need help."

I was promoting a Jay Blackfoot Blues Concert at the Boutwell, but was also selling tickets at Tiny Tots, cross-marketing to direct traffic, which could possibly bring in business, as a lot of elderly guests had driven down from Gaston, and the Boutwell had sold out of tickets.

Tiny Tots was the only place left to get tickets, so Tiny Tots was packed. Guests browsed the store and decided to do some early Easter shopping while one of my two salespersons ran the cash register. When I stepped to the counter, one elderly woman was giving a description of someone, "... She was so pretty and sweet. She was here the last time we came. She helped you pick out that suit for your grandbaby. ..."

She became frustrated when none of the women in her group remembered.

"... She looked about 17. Her name was as pretty as she was." She was describing Melody, who was trying to get the lady to acknowledge her. "Hi, Mrs. Watts. It's me, Melody. I'm right here! ... Daddy, why is she ignoring me?"

I couldn't speak.

My salesperson tried to whisper. "She passed in December."

The ladies couldn't believe it. "Nooo! Nooo! How nice and smart and sweet she was."

Melody had started screaming at me, "Make them stop saying that! I'm here, Daddy! I'm not dead! I'm not dead! I'm here, Daddy! Make them stop! Please?"

My salesperson saw the tears in my eyes that I was fighting to control, then quickly gave the ladies their tickets and the items they'd bought.

Melody had been taken from me quicker than Ivy, but the pain wasn't any less. Her car had hydroplaned on the highway and gone over the rail, falling 50 feet, killing her instantly.

Chapter 12
Distraction

Pearl had started sleeping naked again. We hadn't slept naked since the girls were old enough to get in bed with us. Her goal was to get me to give her emotional reassurance. She needed to feel a closer sense of intimacy. But I'd pulled back into my own world after Melody's death.

My mind wouldn't allow my body to function right. Ivy was in bed with us, cuddled under me, while Pearl was nestling close to me, trying to position herself so our bodies fit as one.

"Not right now. Nooo!"

Pearl's stern look of frustration said it all while she just lay there, staring, remembering the years when our relationship was pure magic, crying to herself, realizing we weren't on the same wavelength as the earlier years. Once I started snoring, Pearl took matters into her own hands, giving me head while I slept, then mounted me, taking what she felt was hers. I awoke to her riding me, thinking I was dreaming until I saw Ivy crying as she ran out of our bedroom.

"Stop. Stop!" I literally had to shove her off of me.

She expressed her feelings openly, "Damn it, Devin! We've got to do something! Something to get us back on track."

She was trying to get me to acknowledge our lives had changed, our relationship had changed. I wasn't ready to admit it. "What are you talking about?"

"I want to have another child."

The pain started in my head. I could hear Ivy crying from her room.

"We can't blame ourselves for their deaths."

I didn't respond. I just got out of bed and went to Ivy's bedroom and cuddled up in bed with her, rocking her, comforting her. "Mommy wasn't hurting daddy. We weren't fighting."

Ivy had walked in once and caught Pearl and me making love when we'd thought she and her sister were asleep: they'd started crying, thinking we were fighting, hurting one another.

Pearl stood at Ivy's bedroom doorway with tears in her eyes, but wouldn't enter.

The following evenings, Pearl buried herself in charity events and volunteered with Belle and April, helping at Jackson Wallace's campaign office, anything to distract her from her loneliness.

Chapter 13
Charisma

Jackson Wallace's campaign promises and the effects of the hardship caused by the failing economy had galvanized the community behind him. His campaign offices had sprouted up all over the city, from plush areas to the hardest of hoods -- people volunteering to help bring change for the better.

Every female in my family was participating in getting Jackson Wallace elected. My mother, my wife, my sister-in-law Belle, April, and Jasmine were all at the campaign headquarters.

Jackson Wallace made sure to make his rounds to all his campaign grassroots' offices, showing his appreciation and encouraging his supporters to continue their efforts.

"This is great. I see why people are being so generous...." staring, somewhat amazed but being charming and flirtatious, using compliments as payment to the mostly female volunteers,

"I'm so mesmerized by all the beautiful people I would drop my entire wallet."

Jackson Wallace flashed his million-dollar smile, speaking to all of them but no one directly, a politician at all times but a womanizer at heart. His eyes fell upon Jasmine, just as tall as Belle, not as thick, but her body was as provocative, firm, and perky. He saw her naivety, the way she stared starry-eyed at him.

"Are you old enough to vote?"

"No."

"Do you mind if I ask how they tricked you into spending this beautiful day inside at my campaign office?" He'd deflected attention from himself, focused it on her, aimed it at her vanity, and stroked her self-esteem, made her feel important.

Jasmine's schoolgirl paparazzi showed when she smiled and blushed.

"No one tricked me. I'm highly interested in politics and didn't want to miss an opportunity to gain experience."

Jasmine and A.J. were my family's future, the next generation, and we all took pride in being a part of their guidance, especially my mother.

"My baby is going to be the governor one day."

"The President, Grandma."

Jackson Wallace took a few seconds just staring at Jasmine, being dramatic so that it appeared he was contemplating something special, which he actually was.

"If you're 100 percent committed, I have a personal assistant position available, but it only pays minimum wage if you accept."

"I'm here for free now! Yes, I accept!"

"Don't you think you should discuss this with your parents first?" He eyed Belle, who was proudly smiling back at her daughter's questioning eyes.

"Yes, but you're not quitting your dance classes, your daddy paid the entire year, and if your GPA drops –"

"It won't, Mom, I promise."

"As long as you know my conditions, I'm fine with it."

Jasmine hugged Belle while smiling at Jackson Wallace.

"Good, you start tomorrow at five."

Chapter 14
Pride

Jasmine had allowed Angel to talk her into going out celebrating with A.J. and Monte. She was somewhat disappointed when Monte wasn't in the car. A.J. had sympathy for both his sister's and his friend's feelings.

"He drove his own car. He wasn't sure you were coming."

Angel coached her. "C'mon. He'll be there."

Jasmine got into the backseat and watched as Angel cuddled up to A.J. as he drove to a nearby community. One of the students' parents worked late at night, so they were having a get-together- a couple's thing, a few jocks, cheerleaders, and band members, eating pizza, drinking, and relaxing to music. Monte was the only one there stag, but Misty and her feminine date, Curtis, were keeping him company when Angel, A.J. and Jasmine entered.

"I told you she was coming."

"Is she really?" Misty's smirk went with the subtext, but Monte hadn't read either.

"She's here."

Misty enviously watched him.

"That's not what I meant."

Monte was somewhat confused, still didn't get it, but walked away anyway. He greeted A.J. with a pound, then kissed the cheek of Angel but passionately kissed Jasmine.

Misty's jealousy made her upstage them, become the center of attention,

"Since everybody is finally here, let's play truth or dare. Curtis, clear the table, put it on the floor."

Curtis did as told, placed the candles and centerpiece on the floor while the others gathered around the table, all but Jasmine.

"C'mon. It'll be fun." Monte tried to get Jasmine to join him at the table.

"No thank you." Jasmine was too mature and was upset when Monte entered the circle around the table.

Misty held an empty beer bottle as she explained the rules,

"...We're going to spin the bottle, and whoever it lands on has to answer a question or accept the dare."

Before Misty could spin the bottle, another girl's question stopped her,

"Why do you get to go first?"

Misty gave her a how dare you look,

"Whoever the bottle lands on gets to go first."

The bottle stopped in the direction of a guy who spent it again, and it stopped closest to Curtis.

"How many times have you and Misty done it?" His girlfriend elbowed him. He so-called whispered to her, but everyone heard, "...He's not going to answer it, because he's gay."

"He's not gay."

Curtis was obviously offended, "I'm not answering because I can't remember."

"Yeah, right. The dare is for you to tongue kiss Liz."

The boy's girlfriend only frowned at him as Curtis approached her, then pulled her into him for a passionate kiss that hushed the room. Curtis released her, then gritted on the guy.

"We used to do this all the time when we were freshmen. When we dated."

"I told you he wasn't gay."

"My turn!" Curtis interrupted with a smile, then spent the bottle which landed on Monte.

"Ole Monte! My man. Truth or dare: Are you a virgin?"

Monte was, but to know him, you wouldn't have thought it. His proud smirk said no, but when the others somewhat glanced in Jasmine's direction, he knew the question also affected her.

"I'll take the dare."

"You will?"

"Yeah."

"Alright, go upstairs in the bedroom with Misty for 15 minutes or tell the truth."

Jasmine and everyone awaited an answer. Once Monte's hand extended toward Misty, Jasmine stepped to her brother.

"I'm ready to go now!"

A.J. was gritting on Monte, who was walking up the stairs with Misty.

"Let's go."

Jasmine didn't say a word the entire ride to her house. A.J. got out behind Jasmine,

"Are you all right?"

"I'm fine. Thanks for bringing me home. I'll see you tomorrow."

She was really hurt and cried herself to sleep until the lights around her home lit up the grounds, and rocks started hitting her window. Monte was outside her window.

"What?"

"I only went upstairs because I didn't want to embarrass you."

"But going upstairs with her didn't! You weren't thinking of me!"

Belle opened the front door of the house with her gun in her hand.

"If you don't get your ass away from her window, I'm going to shoot the shit out of you."

By the first period of school, the news of Misty and Monte going upstairs to the bedroom and having sex had gone viral through the school. Jasmine's entire day was filled with stares and snickers.

Monte met her at her locker.

"We didn't have sex."

Jasmine didn't say a word. She only slapped his face, then walked off.

Jasmine arrived early at the campaign headquarters and sat outside of Jackson Wallace's office. The door was partially open. The male secretary was on the phone. Jasmine could see Jackson Wallace and his wife having a heated discussion.

"You don't understand."

"I understand enough. This is the last straw. I've put up with this shit way too long."

Jackson Wallace's wife was too pissed to even notice the embarrassed expression on Jasmine's face but nothing had escaped Jackson Wallace's eyes. After his wife stormed out, he fanned Jasmine into his office. His anger subsided once Jasmine stood. The navy skirt suit that she had on was very professional but also extremely sensual.

"Close the door behind you, please." His tone carried a weary pitch, but he was actually weighing the situation to see how he could sway it to his advantage.

"I'm sorry you had to see that emotional display. After all these years, she still doesn't understand politics. ... Your first lesson: Politics is consuming. It consumes your entire life. ... Do you have a boyfriend?"

"I did, but not anymore."

"Good, because politics has to come first, for the good of the people must be your first priority. A boyfriend or a wife can be selfish, so they can't understand what is being done, which will be good not only now, but for several generations to come. They don't understand that politicians show intimacy differently from regular people. Okay, down to business. I'm going to bounce my speeches off you; if they can keep you excited, I can only imagine how enthused the crowd will be …"

Jasmine silently sat there admiring him.

"Unless I tell you we're going out on the campaign trail, you can wear your school uniform …"

Chapter 15
I'm Just the Messenger

My mother, Viola, and Belle had been calling me, asking about my brother's whereabouts. It had gone on for close to a week. They knew the only reason my brother would have his phone turned off was that either he was brainstorming, gambling, or in the midst of making money. But they continued to bug me,

"Have you heard from him yet?"

Amere had secluded himself at a farm outside of Warrior, actually training alongside his street fighters, demonstrating take-down moves with a karate instructor, getting tossed around hard, but bounced back up quickly, catching the instructor with a solid hook to the kidney, then sweeping the feet from under the instructor, who fell hard.

Amere was set to attack,

"This's street fighting. Not a karate match." The instructor went over the moves again, but this time showed the quickest entry position for submission once Amere was on the ground.

Amere was with his pits watching Coop run them through the obstacle course when I unexpectedly arrived.

"If I wanted to be bothered, my cell wouldn't be off."

"I know, but they're worrying, Mom. Now she's worried about you. She wants to hear your voice or see you herself to make sure you're fine." Amere stopped in his tracks and gritted at me as if I was the one making the demand.

"I'm just the messenger."

Amere leaned back against the fence and again started staring at Coop with the dogs.

"Why don't you just give Belle the attention she wants?"

The only time they fought was when Belle felt neglected; any other time, she was the most adoring wife to him.

Amere's grit showed his disappointment, his frustration.

"Have the shrink helped you start back to fucking Pearl?"

What I didn't tell Annette, I'd confided in my brother. He wasn't supposed to throw it back in my face, and he knew it.

"I'm sorry. ... I didn't hit Belle. The damn woman is getting crazier, ..." He took a swallow of the milk of magnesia like he was drinking a soda.

"She's given me ulcers."

"What did Doc say?"

"No one is putting their finger up my ass and live."

"They test you through your blood." I made the doctor's appointment for him myself because I knew he wouldn't have.

"Mom said she wants you to take her to A.J.'s baseball game."

Chapter 16
Opportunity on The Table

April had reached out and used her resources to network for Belle, with their sorority sister, Direna Boley, one of the founders of Urban Union Savings and Loans. Belle was dressed especially for the power lunch. Both her and Direna's style and sophistication showed their wealth when Direna stood and shook Belle's hand.

"Mrs. James?"

"Yes. Thank you Ms. Boley, for meeting with me."

A slight rub of the hand, then a touch of the face as a reply, and both ladies' eyes lit up with joy.

"Soror."

"Spring of '89."

"Fall of '89."

The restaurant was an upscale steakhouse, an exclusive establishment.

"... Eli and April speak highly of you."

"Eli? How did he know to give –"

"He's a good friend of mine. Once he found out I was opening another branch, he actually mentioned your name before April came to me. ..."

Belle hadn't given any indication at work that she was considering leaving and became a little anxious but continued listening.

"I'm impressed by your years of loyalty to First Alabama. But I also know they have a Boy Scout system in play when it comes to branch managers."

"Ms. Boley, with that said, does Eli know of our meeting?"

"Believe me, Eli can keep a secret. I'm willing to top your current salary by $7,000 a year and give you access to two time-shared vacation homes. One is in Miami, Florida, and the other is in Boulder, Colorado. And your benefits and retirement will follow you."

"You know my salary?"

"Mrs. James, I know what all the bank managers are making, and what perks they're offered or not."

"Mrs. Boley, I'm not sure this is enough to make me leave my current position." Belle had started feeling an eerie sensation.

Direna smirked, then just flat-out laughed. "Mrs. James, the highest I'm willing to go to have your services is an additional $10,000 to your current salary. ..." Belle sat silently, thinking, wondering why the feeling felt so familiar. "... If you pass up this opportunity, it could be extremely counter-productive to your career or self-destructive, which is usually the same thing."

Direna's words woke Belle up to the fact that she was her own worst enemy, not only in her business career but in her overall life. A discovery Belle wanted to avoid, to shield herself from her unhappiness, but Belle didn't have the strength and conviction to step out of the norm.

"I'm going to need time to think it over and discuss it with my husband."

"Fine. So I'll hear from you before the week is out. Look over your menu, my treat."

"I'm so overwhelmed, I can't eat. But thank you."

On Belle's drive home, the resentment she harbored toward Amere grew, ate at her. Why couldn't she just walk away from him? No one was home, for a good reason, it was only one o'clock in the afternoon. She poured herself a tall drink of rum and pineapple juice, downed it, then poured another. Tears of anguish rolled down her face. She felt duped, fooled taken in by phony promises, sweet talk, and Amere's damn charm.

But the tears were because she hated the fact that she loved him.

Belle had stripped down to her underwear when she heard the front door close. Before she could step to the door of the bedroom, Amere was entering, looking suspicious. He didn't say anything, but she noticed how he was eyeing the room.

"You've been missing for a fuckin' month, and you're sniffing around here for somebody else?" Belle had no shame in being naked.

"Big dick Larry! C'mon out from under the bed. He caught us!"

"Don't play with me. Why are you not at work?"

"I quit."

"Good, I didn't like you slaving anyway."

Belle punched him, caught him off guard, and knocked him to the bed. "Where the fuck have you been?" Then dove on top of him, straddling him, trying to punch him in the face, but he grabbed both of her wrists. Belle was furious, "Muthafucka, I thought you were dead, lying in some alley with your brains blown out!"

She was crying and struggling to punch Amere. He managed to roll her over, landing between her legs while struggling to pin her arms above her head. He became more stern, finally using his weight to totally pin her.

"Stop!"

"I hate you! I hate you! Where have you been?"

He released her arms, but she immediately started swinging at his face. So, he pinned her again. "I know what you want."

"Fuck you!"

To silence her, he tried kissing her, but she kept moving her head from side to side and then started biting at his face. He took control of both her wrists with one hand, while using his free hand to undo his belt and pants.

"I know what you want."

"Fuck you!"

When he entered her, she instantly stopped struggling and wrapped her legs around him, locking them on the back of his thighs, rolling her body to meet his rhythm.

"Yes, baby. Yes!"

Once her hands were released, she unbuttoned and removed his shirt without disturbing his groove. Her hands massaged the muscles in his neck, his back, down to the curve of his ass.

When Belle awoke, she was alone in bed, and the house was completely empty. Pissed was an understatement. It was only 5:30 in the evening. She threw on her sweats but drove past the gym. She rode aimlessly and ended up at a hole-in-the-wall eatery in Ensley.

The hood atmosphere did Belle good, seeing and hearing people truly expressing what they were feeling.

Belle was alone at a table for two, enjoying her soul food and beer, when Preston stepped to her table. He was still debonair. He looked Puerto Rican, a shade of honey with salt and peppered wavy hair.

"Wow, God has truly blessed you."

"If you're trying to fuck, keep it moving, Preston."

"I'm not that man anymore," he tugged at the preacher's collar around his neck.

"That keeps it from getting hard." Belle was referring to Preston becoming a preacher.

"Except with my wife. ..." He sat with his to-go order. "... I haven't seen you here in a long time."

It was the place they'd met 19 years earlier and started a short-lived affair. He was the only other man Belle had ever been with.

"I didn't feel like cooking and wanted something different." Belle could see the hunger in his eyes.

"You are still beautiful. How's Amere?"

"The last time I saw him, he was fine." Her expression showed her grief.

"If you need to, you can always call me."

"I told you I'm not trying to -"

"I'm a preacher now. I provide marriage counseling. Invite Amere as well. Here's my card. So beautiful. Call me." Then he left her alone again.

Chapter 17
Seduction of Power

Jackson Wallace knew what he was doing when he took Jasmine along with him to the meetings with the business owners, with the teachers' union, and with the preachers. He saw how star-struck she was while he spoke, amazed how each group easily agreed to his goodwill,

"... I'll suspend business tax as long as you employ more than a thousand people. ... As long as the students' grades continue to improve, I'll back every pay increase that comes across my desk. .... A moral present is missing from our society, our everyday life, and my administration will create events, programs, and registration to restore this effort."

Not only had Jackson Wallace seduced the group, but Jasmine as well. He'd only dangled the prize before their eyes, suggesting things he knew that the groups already wanted to hear, then allowed their mind to do the rest. He had the ability to lead people to the interpretation without saying. It was an art he'd developed over years of being a prosecutor, such as the goodbye hugs he'd started giving Jasmine before the limo would drop her off at home, which soon included a non-threatening kiss on the cheek.

He knew he had to possess her mind before moving to conquer her body. Jackson Wallace's success became a powerful aura. Jasmine knew anyone could make promises, but what set Jackson Wallace apart, and made him more charming to her; was his ability to come through in the end, follow up his promises with definite actions; being an active member of the city council, he was able to put forth legislation, push already existing bills and programs. Jasmine was right beside him, seeing his actions. It appealed to her confidence and her sexuality, which made his move from mentor to friend to lover seem like it wasn't a maneuver but natural.

Jackson Wallace and Jasmine were alone in his office at his campaign headquarters, going over his speech when his secretary stepped in,

"Everything's locked up. I'm going, boss."

"Fine. We'll be right behind you. ... Which speech do you like the best?"

"Yours."

"They're both mine, young lady."

"The one you wrote!"

"Why?"

"The other one has too much filler, beating around the bush. It's too soft to believe you're being sincere."

Jackson Wallace gazed at her, speechless, just smiling at her.

"What?" Jasmine was impressed.

"That's exactly what I was thinking."

"They say great minds think alike."

"I hope so." Then he passionately kissed Jasmine before she could speak. It was what she'd been dreaming of. Once she responded, kissing him back, he raised her onto the edge of his desk. She was still dressed in her school uniform, so her skirt revealed her laced panties. Their kissing was intense. Jackson Wallace had her panties down to her knees when she grabbed his hand.

"Don't you want this to happen?" Jackson Wallace's voice was calm and comforting, but he was controlling his anxiousness.

"Yes."

"What's wrong?"

"I'm a virgin."

No words, Jackson Wallace just tongued her, then went down on her.

Within seconds, her nails were clawing into the oak desk top, then she reclined all the way back on the desk as Jackson Wallace held her firmly, burying his face between her legs. She was gasping for air, unable to scream out in pleasure as her body seized, and she had no control for what seemed like an eternity.

Jackson Wallace rose, and on the desk top, he made her a woman, adding another conquest to his belt.

Jasmine was in her bedroom, lying across her bed, glowing in the aftermath of her consummation into womanhood, chatting away with Angel on her cell phone,

"… It was great!"

"You finally gave Monte some!"

"Noooo!"

"Who!"

"I can't tell you. But I can give you the details."

"This is too juicy. I'll be over in a minute." Angel only lived three homes over, so she was literally over to Jasmine's, knocking on the door in seconds.

She entered Jasmine's room and dove on the bed next to her,

"Why can't you tell me who he is?"

Jasmine only made faces.

"He has a girlfriend?"

Jasmine's face tightened even more.

"He's married! You're fucking a married man?"

Jasmine quickly covered Angel's mouth.

"My mom can hear you! … Yeah, but his wife is leaving him. She doesn't understand politics."

Angel had to contain her excitement, talking through her closed lips.

"Ooh! You're fucking fine ass Jackson Wallace!"

"Yes! That's why we have to be discreet, and no one else can know."

"I promise I won't tell anybody. Tell me! Tell me everything!"

"He ate me out!"

Angel's jealousy made her mad.

"A.J. ain't getting any more until he eats me!"

Chapter 18
Shattered Innocence

Imagine arriving home from a long day's work to see your lawn destroyed with car tracks going across it in every direction and litter everywhere.

You're not sure what to think.

The inside was even worse, with trash everywhere and a few broken things.

Then you remembered your valuables, your jewelry. A mad dash to the bedroom. The jewelry was still in its place, but reflecting in the mirror was the image of a nude girl lying across the bed.

Forensic agents were taking fingerprints off plastic cups when Ellis Collins entered the crime scene.

An officer was questioning the owner of the home, who seemed fatigued but also sympathetic. The officers noticed Ellis Collins approaching,

"Thank you, sir, for your cooperation. I'm going to have to ask you to step outside until–"

"Just make sure to close the door behind you all."

Ellis Collins waited as the officer flipped through his notepad to the first page.

"It's the same M.O. as the others." The officer was referring to the other skip parties.

"He's divorced and now lives alone. He has no idea who the girl is."

"Where's the body?"

In the bedroom, one agent was going through the girl's clothes on the floor beside the bed. Inside one of the jeans' pockets was the girl's school ID card and driver's license. She attended the same school as Ellis Collins' daughter.

Another agent was using a violent light to detect semen samples on the sheets of the bed.

Ellis Collins stared in silence for a few seconds, envisioning Ebony lying dead in the bed, then angrily snapped out of it,

"Make sure to dust those for prints." Referring to the cups on the nightstands.

Ellis Collins' car pulled curbside in front of a moderate-income home in a decent subdivision of Lakeshore. It matched the address on Lisa Givens' license.

As Ellis Collins approached the front door, he could see a boy and a girl playing video games. The family resemblance was obvious. Then came the part of his job he hated, but it had to be done, and it wasn't an easy way to do it.

The boy answered the door. He was probably no older than 12.

"Mom, there's a man at the door!"

His sister, a step taller than he was, came to the door behind him, staring.

The mother approached, moving them out of the way,

"Have you all finished your homework?"

They both silently backed away, then she focused on Ellis Collins,

"How can I help you?" She was pleasant and cheerful, and he was about to deliver news that would change her life forever.

"Mrs. Givens?"

"Yes."

"Is Mr. Givens' home?"

She became a little concerned,

"Yes. What is this concerning?"

"I'm Detective Collins. May I come in?"

"Willie! Willie, come down here!" She stared at Ellis' badge before opening the burglar door, allowing him in.

"You guys go to your room. Now."

Willie Givens was a big man, as big as Ellis Collins. His wife answered his questioning eyes.

"This is Detective Collins. This is my husband."

"You have a daughter named Lisa Givens?"

"Yes."

"She should be home any second..." She saw the compassion in Ellis's eyes, "...Why are you asking about my baby?"

"Calm down, babe," The husband tried to settle his wife, though Ellis Collins' questions rattled him, too. "She's probably just got in a little trouble. Our daughter is a good girl. She has had straight A's her entire life. If she's gotten into anything, it's her boyfriend's doing. What has he gotten our baby into?"

"I'm so sorry Lisa's body was discovered earlier this evening."

The mother instantly started screaming,

"Noooo! Noooo! God, please!"

Her husband hugged her, trying to console her, while in somewhat shock himself,

"How do you know it's our daughter?"

Ellis Collins handed him the school ID and license, and the tears rolled down the father's face.

"I'ma kill him."

"Mr. and Mrs. Givens, the time may be inappropriate, but I need you to answer some questions so I can stop this from happening to another child."

"Was my baby raped?"

"No, sir. An overdose."

"My baby didn't do drugs or drink! She was a good girl!"

"I'm not suggesting she wasn't. Do you know of any of her associates who might've used drugs or had access to drugs?"

"Only Caesar! I'ma kill him!"

"Mr. Given, I can't imagine yours or your family's pain. ..." He saw the tears in the boy and girl's eyes while the mother clutched onto Mr. Givens. "... Allow the law to handle this. Your family needs you. ... Where can I find Caesar?"

It was dark and late, a dangerous time for anyone to be roaming around the Brickyard, a set of government projects, especially a law enforcer. The project was the location where Lisa Givens' late grandmother lived, two doors down from where Mr. Givens believed Caesar lived.

Ellis Collins wasn't about to allow the opportunity to solve the case pass not if it meant he could get closer to catching the person dealing drugs to children, killing the children. Ellis Collins knocked on the door, not knowing if he should allow his badge to hang from his jacket pocket or not. He decided to put it away.

An elderly woman opened the door slowly, gritting at him,

"What do you want at this time of night?"

"I'm looking for Caesar."

The door opened wider, but the woman stepped out in her house robe, shouting at the apartment directly across the street, where several youngsters were gathered drinking beer, listening to rap music.

"Caesar, if another muthafucka wakes me up looking for your skinny ass, I'ma call the damn police on you my damn self! ... Get your ass off my stoop!"

Neither of the boys said a word, but their body language changed, and they became defensive. Ellis Collins confidently but cautiously crossed the street, scanning the boys, detecting the thinnest out of the crowd.

"Yo Caesar, let me holla at you."

As if Ellis Collins' voice gave a warning that he was a policeman, all the boys ran in different directions. Ellis Collins chased after the thinnest one. He was gaining until Caesar ran into an apartment, straight through the front door, passed the old sleeping lady, and jumped over the little children who were lying on the floor watching wrestling. Ellis Collins did the exact same thing, except the woman had awakened and was screaming at them,

"I'ma get Bug to beat both y'all asses when he gets home from work!"

Shots were fired as soon as Ellis Collins opened the back door; chunks of bricks flew out of the side of the apartment.

Ellis Collins knew the area; he'd been raised, one community over, Pratt City, when he was young. The Brickyard was his stomping grounds, so he knew that at the end of the set of apartments was a dead end, a laundry room with no exit.

Ellis Collins moved silently, listening, his gun drawn, easing clothes to the side that hung from the clothes lines as he made his way toward the laundry room. Then he stopped. He didn't want Caesar to feel trapped. If all the apartments were locked, the only other option would be to try to climb the 12-foot fence that divided the brickyard from the rest of Ensley's main street.

"I just want to talk to you about Lisa! I–" Shots rang out, and Ellis Collins had to duck down to the ground.

Caesar was running for the fence. Ellis Collins had a bead on him but didn't pull the trigger,

"Stop! I just want to question you!"

Caesar was half the way over the fence when he raised his gun in Ellis Collins' direction. Two quick shots exploded from Ellis Collins' gun, both rounds hitting Caesar in the chest. The weight of Caesar's limp body was impaled on the spiked rods on the top of the fence.

"Goddamnit! I just wanted to talk to you!"

The time was 3:45 am when Ellis Collins entered his home. It was dark and silent. Instead of going to his bedroom, he entered his daughter's bedroom and turned the light on, awakening her.

"Dad!" She sat up and watched as her father ransacked her room.

"Dad, what are you doing?"

Ellis Collins was wide-eyed and sweating when he finally stopped.

"Do you know about the skip parties? Have you been to one?"

"No!"

"Do you do drugs?"

"No! What's the big deal about the skip parties?"

"The big deal is Lisa Givens, Adrian Parks, Jackie Johnson, and Candace Pollard are all dead, OD'd at skip parties! All students at your school."

"Lisa is dead?" Her tears didn't soften her father.

"What do you know about these skip parties?"

Ellis Collins' mother-in-law stepped to the bedroom door in her house robe.

"Why are you screaming at her?" Then sat on the bed, consoling Ebony. "Lisa was her friend."

"I don't want it to happen to any more of her friends or her! ... Ebony, what do you know about the skip parties?"

"They're posted online!"

"What?"

"Go to Facebook or Twitter. Each school has an account."

Ellis Collins was looking at Ebony's laptop, but couldn't believe how bold and tech-savvy the children were.

"How do you know the location?"

"It's just floating around the school. Dad. I promise I don't do drugs, and I haven't been to a skip party."

Ellis Collins hugged her tightly and fought back his tears while staring at his mother-in-law.

Ellis Collins and Annette were closer than they would admit. He entered her office a little past noon.

"We had a lunch date?"

"Not officially, but–"

"Let me grab my things. My next appointment isn't until two." She turned to see Ellis Collins sitting on the couch, looking off into space.

"... Is this a session visit?"

"Not really, but yeah. We're more than just sex, right?" They'd been dating for three years.

"Yes. Is our relationship what has you spaced out?"

"Not only. Do you feel like I'm smothering you?"

"No. Where is this coming from?" She sat beside him.

Ellis Collins felt her warmth and support. He loved her and would've been married to her if it was only him. But he had his mother-in-law and daughter to think of. He didn't know if they were ready to see him in love with another woman.

"I don't want to smother the ones I love. But I have to protect y'all." Annette caught the L-word. It made her feel good, but she quickly converted to a therapist,

"Is the ecstasy case–"

"Yes. One of Ebony's friends and four of her schoolmates overdosed."

"Ebony's a smart girl. You've done a great job raising her. Now you have to trust her."

"I'm scared if I lose her, I'll lose it." He hadn't introduced her to his family, but he'd discussed them with her, so that she felt as if she knew them.

Chapter 19
Open Mic

Jackson Wallace knew how valuable Ira Battle's endorsement was to his campaign. Ira was his connection to the gay community, which would assure the mayor's election for him.

Ira wasn't gay, but was the unofficial ambassador, his club, his events, catered to and openly accepted the gay community. The new age of thinking hadn't reached the black community. To be openly gay or support the lifestyle was, for most, a death sentence to one's career, even in entertainment.

Still, Jackson Wallace had strategically risked going to Ira's club to court his endorsement.

It was open-mic Wednesday, the night of the largest crowd of the week.

Jackson Wallace knew that even if Ira didn't endorse him, word of him being there would sway some to believe he was at least open-minded to the gay community.

"…What would you have me say to them on your behalf?"

Jackson Wallace had become a little impatient with Ira.

"The same thing our greatest president said. When the tide rises, all the ships on it rise. Jobs are coming. If they qualify, companies can't discriminate. I'm pushing for a safer environment, which includes safety for all. And you and everyone else know how hard I'm fighting to upgrade our school district to help all children. Me being the mayor is beneficial to all."

"Why can't you just meet with them and personally address their issues?"

Jackson Wallace smirked as he inhaled and exhaled, giving himself time to detach and think clearly.

"If they're brave enough to attend my next open town hall meeting, I'll openly discuss their issues. We all want transparency. Extend my invitation to them."

Jackson Wallace and Ira knew he'd checkmated Birmingham's gay community; it would be too much media coverage, exposure to a degree of a death blow.

......

Pearl, Belle, and April felt their marriages or relationships had become boring and disappointing, dull and mundane and were annoyed with me, Doc, and Amere. They'd all agreed to a ladies' night out, which landed them at Ira's club for open mic.

The club was packed; the singers who had entered the contest were excellent, all jazz singers.

Pearl, Belle, and April were relaxing with their drinks, which opened them up to more honestly venting about their issues.

"... He's not touching me either. ... I'd done my best to maintain our marriage. Keeping him together emotionally. What he's putting me through was most definitely 'not' in our vows."

"That's the alcohol talking. Both of you love being married. So shut up. As soon as you get some, it'll be all lovey-dovey again."

Pearl ignored April with a stare, then focused on Belle,

"I know how you feel; you can't understand how something so right can go so terribly wrong?"

April poured the last of the champagne into Pearl and Belle's flutes

"Drink. Be quiet. You're making it sound worse than what it really is."

April was still romantically in love with Doc, but was upset at the fact that he hadn't proposed yet.

"Just wait. You and Doc are in love now. Fuckin' like rabbits. You find him so intriguing, and he's so interested in you and everything you do. It all changes once you say I do."

"Shut up, Belle!"

"Fine. Find out for yourself."

Guys were approaching their table, somewhat interrupting their chat session.

Belle annoyingly fanned them away.

"We're just here to enjoy the music."

One of the guys returned to his table and flagged down a waitress, who left and returned with a bottle of champagne and the flower man.

The guy had a flair to him.

"Count how many roses are in the bucket for me. I don't trust him."

Once the waitress began counting the roses, the guy had two ecstasy pills and was about to drop them into the champagne flutes but didn't when the waitress turned toward him.

"17."

The guy paid the waitress and the flower man from a large stack of cash, then tipped the waitress a $100 bill.

"Deliver these to that table. Make sure you tell them it's from me."

As soon as the bottle of champagne and roses were delivered, April's cell started ringing. She started screaming hysterically once she put it to her ear, then calmed herself when she noticed the people staring at her.

"Yes! Yes! As soon as Angel graduates."

April was somewhat in shock as she noticed Doc approaching through the club.

When Doc got to the table, he immediately went down on one knee. Belle and Pearl's eyes watered instantly, showing their happiness for their friends' relationship, then they were saddened thinking about their own.

Belle's cell rang, and she seemed somewhat surprised when she read the caller ID.

"What is this about? ... You were? Really? ... I do. ... Now? ... I'll meet you there."

Doc and April were leaving when Belle ended her call and stood.

"What's up?" Pearl was about to stand also.

"I have to make a run. It'll be quick."

"You want me to come?"

"Noooo! I'll be right back. I promise."

Then Belle left, leaving Pearl somewhat dumbfounded.

The guy who had sent the roses and champagne was closely eyeing Pearl's table, watching her sitting alone, just enjoying the music. He approached the table and sat with an admiring smirk, then refilled her flute while dropping two ecstasy pills in the flute and one in the bottle without her noticing.

"Your friends left you?"

"Seems that way. Thank you for the champagne and roses."

"My pleasure. I'm Bachi."

"I'm Pearl."

"Wow, truly a rare find. Do you really know how beautiful you are?"

Pearl was unconsciously smiling, obviously enjoying what she was hearing while drinking the champagne.

"Would you like to dance?"

Pearl's question was unexpected, and it showed in Bachi's expression.

"I don't dance. I've got two left feet."

"That's too bad. I would love to." Jackson Wallace interrupted, extending his hand to Pearl. His smile was irresistible.

Bachi recognized Jackson Wallace and bowed out gracefully.

Jackson Wallace had all the right moves. He and Pearl were the center of attention, stepping and walking the floor for four consecutive songs. But when a slow song came on, Pearl led the way back to the table.

She looked great. Her dress lay perfectly loose but sensually accented her curves. Her heels made her strut that much more defiant, an opposing force. Both sat somewhat exhausted and exhilarated.

"Good God, I enjoyed that. I can't remember the last time I danced like this."

Jackson Wallace took it upon himself to refill the flutes in front of them.

"Wow, you can really work it. With moves like yours, I would never want you to stop dancing."

Then he took her hand, simulating as if they were still dancing.

"Devin and I used to dance all the time. I love dancing."

Drinking the last of the champagne in her glass, which Jackson Wallace quickly refilled, emptying the bottle.

"You have the body of a professional dancer. Long, graceful, and so sensuous."

Still holding her hand. He'd made a mental note that she'd used the phrase used to.

"I used to dream of being a Broadway dancer."

"Why didn't you go for it?"

"I fell in love. I was in love."

"Are you still in love?"

"Yes! Yes. I love my Devin."

She snatched her hand back and seemed anxious, looking around.

"I didn't mean–"

"Noooo! The champagne has me tipsy, and Belle hasn't come back. I rode here with her."

"I'm leaving. I'll be happy to give you a ride home. Lakeshore isn't out of my way."

"I wouldn't want to burden you."

"It's nothing, as much as your family is helping with my campaign. C'mon."

Pearl stood and tried to shake off the effects of the champagne.

Jackson Wallace sized her up, putting a hand on the small of her back, helping to steady her.

Once the valet brought the car around, Jackson Wallace helped Pearl into the front seat while somewhat caressing the nakedness of her back, testing the waters.

As they drove through the city streets, soft mood music played.

Pearl seemed fixated on the night lights of the city.

"It takes a strong woman to hold it together after the tragedies you've gone through, then to have to deal with an emotional breakdown from the one you depend on for strength."

He took her hand and put it to his lips, kissing it, holding it there.

The warmth and wetness from his mouth illuminated all sorts of different and contradictory feelings in Pearl.

"You've done your best. You need a relief."

His lips, his words awakened something stranger than usual, stronger than usual. She couldn't understand how his kissing her hand could make her body react in such a dangerous way by not reacting.

Jackson Wallace placed his hand on her thigh and started to massage the inside of her leg with his and her hand. When she didn't stop him, he worked his hand between her legs and explored her, entered her with his finger. Then he detoured, exited the freeway, and pulled into the parking lot of a hotel.

While Jackson Wallace went to the desk, Pearl fumbled with her purse trying to get her cell. Her vision blurred, and by the time she'd gotten her cell, Jackson Wallace was opening her door.

"Put that back before you lose it."

He somewhat forcibly helped her out of the car. Pearl was trying to use her weight to stay outside of the hotel, but Jackson Wallace was too strong,

"You deserve some relief."

The male receptionist was stunned, just staring at them as they got into the elevator.

"A little too much to drink. We're fine."

The ecstasy had Pearl discombobulated, so Jackson Wallace had to almost drag her into the room. She wasn't able to even resist him taking off her dress.

"Stop. Stop." Then fell back on the bed as Jackson Wallace undressed her.

Looking at her lying naked on the bed, the ecstasy had Jackson Wallace feeling in total control, a benign version of the power of lust, sinister and potentially violent sex.

Pearl cried defenselessly, "Stop, stop. No. Noooo."

But Jackson Wallace didn't have the power to stop himself until he was totally exhausted from coming inside her. He rolled off of her.

Pearl's voice was weak, a trembling whisper, "You drugged me and raped me."

"You're a damn lie! I didn't force you!"

Pearl tried to sit up but couldn't. "I said no. You raped me!"

Jackson Wallace was in shock himself, hurrying to get dressed, "You're crazy if you think anyone will believe that. Think how Devin is going to react."

He then left her in the hotel room.

Pearl laid there crying until she could manage to get to her purse and her cell.

"Come get me, please. Please. He raped me."

Pearl had called April, who came in a hurry, but also brought Doc.

"We have to call the police."

Pearl couldn't fight her tears,

"I can't. They won't believe me."

"Why?"

"It was Jackson. It was Jackson."

"Jackson Wallace!"

They took Pearl to Doc's clinic for blood tests and collected semen from her. Pearl returned home at 5:45 in the morning and locked herself in the bathroom, crying to herself.

Chapter 20
Blood in The Water

Amere was about to flush the toilet when he noticed the water was pink.

Once examining the turd closer, he spotted that blood was mixed in with it. It was the forcing point that made him go see Doc.

Doc was also Ellis Collins and Amere sands, so he knew exactly how to handle my brother.

"Stop crying. Nothing is going up your ass today, but if these tests' results show a need for it that's what's happening." Drawing more blood from Amere's arm. "I can't believe you waited this–"

"It's just an ulcer."

"It might be, but we need to find out."

"Can you give me something to coat my stomach until the test comes back?"

Doc gritted his teeth on him, knowing my brother only used medication as a last resort, any other time Amere endured. But Doc wrote the prescription.

"You're going to be my groomsmen."

"I've told you I'm not going to any damn wedding."

"Bro, I ain't hearing your shit. I'm telling you, Sands, you are going to be in my damn wedding. Now let's go buy me a drink. Damn, you can't drink with this."

"I can't anyway. I've got to be somewhere. Next week."

Amere had picked up Mom and taken her to A.J.'s baseball game. Seemed like the entire school was there in support. A.J.'s fastball had been the buzzing news of the city since he'd pitched two back-to-back no-hitters, so fans from all over were there to see if he could keep the streak alive.

Amere spotted the college and pro scouts in the stands. A guy holding a radar gun was outside the gate near the catcher, clocking the speed of each of A.J.'s pitches, shouting "93 miles per hour!" so the crowd could hear.

Mom had been observing Amere, how, after eating his hot dog, he kept burping, then finally drank from his milk-of-magnesia bottle.

"It's just gas. I'm fine."

"You've lost weight. What did Doc say?"

Jasmine came over, and Amere used her to divert the conversation, seeing how short the skirt was of her school uniform.

"You went to school like this!"

"It's our school uniform. Grandma, are you ready to go?"

"It's only three more innings." Grandma focused back on A.J., who was on the mound.

A.J. still hadn't allowed a hit, but Jasmine didn't care.

"I'm going to be late."

"Child, I'm here to support your brother. The election isn't until November."

"You need to go home and change."

"Dad, this is my school uniform!"

"What did I say? I'll drop your grandma off."

The crowd went silent as the echo of the bat connecting with the ball vibrated, and they saw a line drive blast down the third baseline. All eyes quickly darted to the official who signaled fair ball, and A.J.'s streak ended.

"Are you ready now?"

"No! Go do what your dad said. I need to talk to him anyway."

Amere listened but was observing the way his son recovered, pitching even faster, harder,

"94 mph! ... 96 mph! ... 97 mph!"

Striking out the last batter.

"That's my grandbaby! Yeah! ..." My Mother then focused back on Amere, "... You're too old to be still playing with Viola and Belle. Viola is a good woman and needs someone full-time. Don't make her spin her entire life like this. You and Belle need counseling. She loves you to death. So don't make her kill you."

.....

Belle entered her home and was somewhat surprised to see that the only light came from the candles on the table, which was set for a romantic dinner for two.

Amere was in a suit and tie. He greeted her with a kiss and a flute of champagne. Belle was so startled that all she could do was laugh as he escorted her to her seat, then pushed the chair up to the table behind her like a perfect gentleman.

"It's not our anniversary. What's the occasion?"

"The fact we're still together when no one believed we would last."

"They thought we would kill each other."

"I love you."

Those three words got Belle out of her seat. She kissed him with so much desire that they forgot about dinner. She undressed him, there in the dining room. The passion in their touch, in their kiss, their stroke, it was love the right way. Sensual, passionate, caring, a spiritual connection of soul mates. They both were somewhat breathless in each other's arms.

"C'mon. Let's go get into bed."

He then stood but stopped; he didn't want to leave her on the floor.

"C'mon. I've got to use the bathroom. C'mon."

"Gone. I'll be there."

Belle gathered herself, smiling, feeling good all over, then she began picking up Amere's clothes and spotted dried blood in the seat of his boxers.

Belle was walking toward the bathroom door with the boxers when Amere shouted to her,

"If you still want to meet with Preston for marriage counseling, I'll go."

She entered the bathroom with him on the toilet.

"I'll set the appointment."

Then put his underwear in the hamper without mentioning the bloody boxers.

Chapter 21
When Everything Falls Apart

It was less than 45 days away from our annual pre-Easter fashion show, which had started out as a way to promote Tiny Tots' Closet plus local designers. After Ivy had passed, my mother had basically taken over until Melody had talked me back into participating. I couldn't bring myself to stop it after Melody's death. My mom or the church wouldn't allow it to stop anyway. We'd been members of AME when it could only hold 250 people at full capacity. It'd grown to the size of a college campus with 15,000 members, and everything was state-of-the-art.

My mother and I, along with my daughters and our models, were at rehearsal when the Rev, distinguished and in his late 60s, with a silver fade, entered with a woman and 20 children and racks of clothes. No one knew them. On top of that, our models were pretty wannabes with dreams of one day being a supermodel. But as soon as the new children came down the runway, we all knew they were professional models.

I was reading the description of their outfits, and they were all wearing name brands.

My mother had approached the woman,

"So you're a designer?"

"No. I run fashion shows all over the world."

The woman was so arrogant and conceited. But she'd picked the wrong woman to get snobbish with. My mother could be as fierce as the best of alley cats. My mother was the type to come to school, clown the teacher if the teacher was wrong, or beat my brother's or my butt if we were in the wrong. I guess that's why my brother had fallen for Belle, because she reminded us of our mother at an earlier age, but age had given my mother control.

"Whoa. Why are you here?"

"To supervise and help take this annual promotion to the next level."

"Hold that thought. Rev, what in the hell kind of mess are you trying to pull?"

"Sister James, let's remember we're in the house of the Lord."

"Well, why in the hell have you sold your soul to the devil?"

Several major department stores had been trying to buy Tiny Tot's closet for years and had studied our promotion campaign. Tiny Tots was more than brick-and-mortar. We had exclusive deals with designers who had been proven through sales at Tiny Tots.

"Sister James the donations will go farther than anything we'll collect during the fashion show."

"This is my son's fashion show! Without him it won't be a show!"

Melody and Ivy were screaming at me,

"Dad, business is already slow. If he does this, we'll have to sell."

"Daddy, I like being in the fashion show."

With both my girls demanding something from me, I had to calm everyone down.

"We have time. I haven't started advertising. We'll find another venue."

The Rev realized I'd started directing my models toward the door.

"Wait. Wait Devin."

He knew the entertainment was all under contract with Tiny Tots.

"Not now Rev. You run your fashion show, and we'll continue to have ours. Rehearsal is over. I'll call everyone tomorrow about the location and date of our next rehearsal. Let's go, Mom."

I was at home in my study, racking my brain to think of a marketing strategy that no other fashion show could compete with. Pearl was home but was in bed. I thought she was just giving me space.

My girls wouldn't allow me to concentrate.

"Why hasn't Mom come out of the bedroom?"

"Mom didn't cook?"

"Something's wrong with mom."

"Is Mom sick, Dad?"

"Dad, go check on mom."

"Mom's crying, Dad!"

My girls weren't going to allow me to do anything other than check on their mother.

"Your mom is fine. ... If I go check on her, will you two allow me to concentrate?"

"Go, Dad!"

"Please?"

When I entered our bedroom, Pearl's face was puffy like she'd been crying. She looked terrible.

"What's wrong?"

I saw the pain in her face, but she couldn't articulate the words; only more tears came out. I held her and she trembled and cried in my arms.

"Tell me what's wrong."

At first, I didn't understand, then I didn't want to understand.

"I was raped!"

I felt more violated than she did. I couldn't save my daughters, and now I've allowed my wife to be raped.

"By whom?"

She gained some composure.

"Jackson Wallace."

I immediately dug into the dresser drawer and got my 44.

"When?"

"Wednesday."

Things were semi-registering. My rage was clouding my logic.

"Why are you just telling me?"

"Because I didn't know if you would believe me."

She'd gotten out of bed and was blocking my path.

"What! Move!"

"Please. Please let's let the police handle it."

Everything seemed to slow down. Neither one of us spoke during the ride to the police station. A million thoughts were racing through my head along with the rage to kill. Pearl reached over and took my hand and held it tightly.

She didn't release it until it was time to get out at the police station.

I knew the entire police staff from the courtroom and when visiting my clients.

"We need to speak with a lieutenant."

A young lieutenant was signaled over.

"What's the problem?"

"I want to report I was raped."

"Right this way."

As we followed him to his cubicle, his eyes were thoroughly examining Pearl for physical signs.

"Have a seat please."

He quickly logged onto his PC while continuing his questioning

"Did you know the perpetrator?"

Pearl took my hand again.

"Yes. Jackson Wallace."

Instantly the lieutenant's face tightened, his disbelief became obvious.

"Where did this take place?"

Pearl hesitated, squeezing my hand.

"At a hotel."

"At a hotel?"

"He drugged me and forced me."

"How did he drug you?"

"He must have slipped it in my drink at the club."

"You two were at a club having drinks? On a date?"

Pearl was becoming annoyed and frustrated; they were the same questions I'd asked victims when I'd defended accused rapists.

"No! I was there with my girlfriends. He asked me to dance, then joined the table."

"So, he drugged you and forced you to leave, in front of your girlfriends?"

"No. We'd finished our bottle of champagne."

"So, what were you and your girlfriends celebrating?"

"We weren't celebrating. It was a ladies' night out."

"But your girlfriends allowed you to be forced out of a club?"

"No. April left with Doc, and Belle had to make an emergency run."

"So did Mr. Wallace force you to leave the club?"

"No. I was tipsy and felt uncomfortable at the club, so I was about to call a cab and Jackson Wallace somewhat demanded I allow him to drive me home."

"Were you drunk or drugged?"

"I was both!"

"How do you know?"

"Because I had tests run on my blood!"

Pearl's answer added validity to her complaint. The lieutenant's expression showed it also.

"One moment please."

Pearl and I were still holding hands when the lieutenant left. I felt her staring at me. My mind was in lawyer mode, processing the pieces I'd heard but there were gaps that my mind wouldn't allow me to fill or even wanted filled.

The lieutenant returned with a prosecutor. I knew him personally, had gone head-to-head with him many times in the courtroom, and he was a close friend of Jackson Wallace.

"Mr. and Mrs. James I have one more question. It's personal, but I need you to be completely honest with me. Are you two having marital problems?"

"What does this question have to do with the fact I was drugged and raped!"

"When you take the stand, you're not the victim anymore. You are the accuser. Your entire life is open for scrutiny. This is not an ordinary man you're accusing, but a powerful political leader of this city. And the recent tragedy you two have suffered, plus the fact your husband has taken an extended leave of absence–"

"Mr. Sims, are you trying to scare me into not pressing charges?"

"No, Mrs. James, I'm being honest with you and Devin. But if you are intent on filing this complaint, there will be no indictment. I'm sorry about your ordeal."

Then he backed away.

I stood, still holding Pearl's hand. She resisted at first, then stood along with me. From an objective point of view, the complaint was iffy, and whether we said it or not, we did have marital problems.

Pearl stared at me the entire way to the car. I hadn't spoken; I didn't know what I was feeling. I was fumbling with my car's keys when I heard the tremble in her voice.

"Do you believe me?"

Our daughters were in the back seat of the car, both defending their mother.

"Tell her yes, Daddy. Tell her yes."

"Dad, don't make Mom cry."

"Do you believe me? Do you believe me, Devin?"

I didn't answer Pearl because I didn't know.

"Devin, say something!"

"Why did you put yourself in that situation? Why did you go to the club?"

It shocked Pearl that the questions were now coming from me. Her expression was one of disbelief as if I knew better. She remained silent as I drove.

Chapter 22
A Race Against Time.

Facebook and Twitter accounts were registered to real people, but dead people. People who had been dead before Facebook and Twitter even existed.

Ellis Collins was in the captain's office trying to convince him, because the captain was being unreceptive,

"... A sweep of the high school! Have you lost your mind?"

Ellis Collins knew the resistance he would be facing, but he had no choice. He had run into dead ends trying to pin down who was responsible for the skip parties.

"Eleven out of the 14 overdose victims were high school students. If we don't find the source quickly, there will be more."

The captain knew Ellis Collins was right, but he was reluctant about okaying it. This was an election year, and the city was contemplating filing for bankruptcy.

"The mayor's not going to like this."

"Tell her it might be the only shining light of her interim."

"Give me a day or two to explain things to her."

"We don't have a day or two! Even though we shut down the Facebook and Twitter accounts, more have sprouted up broadcasting skip parties..."

The captain's expression was that of a fighter cornered, ready to attack, but the bell had rung, ending the fight.

"Twelve men, four dogs. That's all I need."

"My budget is depleted."

"Eleven men, four dogs?"

"Eight men, three dogs, and you better wrap this up within the month! If you don't, you know both of our heads are on the chopping block."

Ellis Collins started the sweep searches at his daughter's high school. Since it was private and Ellis Collins didn't have a warrant, he had to obtain permission to search from the principal, who understood but was afraid of the backlash.

"I don't know Detective Collins–"

"Principal Adams, four of your students have OD'd within two months. How many more need to die to prove this is needed?"

"Our head of security will accompany your team. Mr. Banks."

From the classroom windows, the students could see the policemen and school security with the dogs in the student parking lot. Some students tried to leave the classrooms to find more policemen and school security with dogs in the hallways, going through each locker.

"Return to your class! If you are needed, you will be called to the principal's office!"

The students obeyed Ellis Collins' order, they all went back to their classrooms, but on their cells.

Within the hour, the principal was beside Ellis Collins,

"My line hasn't stopped ringing. Irate parents, lawyers threatening to sue. News stations' camera crews are on the property filming, waiting for you all to exit. Please tell me you have found something, something to justify this search. Something to show we are trying to make sure this is a safe environment to learn."

"We have, but we're not done. ... If you would, Principal Adams, tell the parents and the lawyers, I'll do a press conference today at the end of the school period."

"Here on this campus!"

"With your permission. Mr. Banks, will you please show Principal Adams what has been discovered while we finish the search?"

Several bags of marijuana, several bottles of ecstasy pills and two handguns were enough to calm Principal Adams' worries.

Exactly at four o'clock, the front entrance of the school was surrounded by angry parents and students and anxious television news crews. On the stairs leading up to the entrance were the principal, the teachers and Ellis Collins.

Principal Adams was trying to calm the crowd.

"Please! Please! There's justification for our actions today. ..."

"You're violating our Fourth Amendment!"

"No. That's not true. Your parents gave this school the right to search you and your property to safeguard you. And with the recent tragic incidents among our student body, I deemed it necessary to allow Detective Collins, who is also the parent of one of our students, to conduct his investigation by searching your lockers and the outside of your vehicles. And several students who have been absent on certain dates will be scheduled for interviews with the school administration and Detective Collins–"

The crowd responded even more rudely and loudly. Principal Adams gritted his teeth at Ellis Collins, who took over the conversation.

"There is an epidemic of overdoses among high school students. Somehow, the misconception of ecstasy pills being harmless and strictly a feel-good party enhancer is killing our children. Predators are preying on our children, making millions of dollars off of our children's consumption of this could be lethal and highly addictive drug!"

He held up the aspirin-sized pill.

"High school is not intended to cradle our children into the prison pipeline but is meant to be a pipeline to a career. We must safeguard our future. That is exactly what our children are. ..."

The crowd humbled, absorbed his message. The parents nodded in agreement.

"Principal Adams will be calling the parents of the students that will be interviewed, so you can be present," Ellis Collins scanned the crowd, then continued.

"The quicker we can stop this predator, the safer our children will be. Thank you for your cooperation."

Chapter 23
High Stakes and Family Bonds

The high school baseball season had ended, and Amere had promised to take A.J. with him the next time he went out of town to gamble on his dogs and street fighters. Amere was the type of father who just didn't tell his children how to do something; he also showed them why and how.

Since Monte was being raised by his mother, Amere had somewhat taken a liking to him, plus there was the fact that Monte was A.J.'s best friend and Jasmine's boyfriend, so Monte got to go out of town with them.

Amere was a man's man with a flair the boys admired and envied. He used it to captivate them while schooling them on all aspects of life,

"Everything you do has to have a purpose or you shouldn't be doing it."

They were in Jackson, Miss, but the location had been changed to Yazoo City, Miss. the middle of nowhere, drained swamp land with bugs as big as birds, but the warehouse was huge with several pits so multiple matches could be held at the same time. The place was packed with people. Major amounts of cash were passing hands.

Eight out of ten of Amere's pitbulls won, and nine out of ten of his street fighters won. In every bout, Amere was damn near in the pit with his men or his dogs, screaming encouragement, coaching, taking side bets. It was truly a bloody sport with high stakes. The boys loved the excitement and especially the amount of cash Amere won.

.....

Belle was at the hole-in-the-wall eatery, at a table for two with Preston. She needed a more distant person to confide in other than Pearl and April. The issue was more personal.

"You think he might be gay because of the blood in his boxers?"

"That could explain it. But if he is, will you still love him?"

Belle answered without hesitation, "Yeah!"

"Why?" Preston seemed hurt.

"Because I know he's not gay. Amere would kill a muthafucka before he gets fucked in the ass."

Preston just sat there shaking his head, watching as Belle continued to eat her meal.

Belle finally looked up, "Oh, before I forget. He agreed to marriage counseling. So make our session the same time next week, but at the church. ..."

Preston's sour expression stunned her.

"... That's a good thing? He wants to make things better."

"Yes. If he really wants to."

.....

Amere didn't turn his cell back on until late Sunday night, when he was back at his Warrior Ranch, putting his dogs back into the kennels.

The weekend had the boys exhausted in the back seat while Amere listened to his messages, deleting most of them after learning who it was from. But once he heard,

"This is Doc. Amere, this is serious. I need you to come in for more tests."

Amere immediately used his voice control. "Call Doc."

"Nupe, do you realize what time it is?"

"You said it was serious. What's what?"

"I don't feel right telling you this over the phone."

"Tell me or I'll come over there."

"Come in for tests in the morning and I'll explain everything."

"Hell naw! You know I won't be able to sleep until I know what's the fuck's going on."

"The tests are showing a possibility of being malignant."

"I've got cancer?"

"I'm not sure. That's why I need you to come in tomorrow to run more tests."

"What kind?"

"An autopsy."

"I thought that was shit you do on dead people."

"It's not. I need to check your colon and your intestines."

"You're not putting your finger up my ass."

"Naw, I'm not. I'm going to put a camera up your ass."

"What type of freak show do you think you're gonna get?"

"Nupe, bring your ass to my office in the morning. Goodnight, Nupe."

Amere wasn't one for waiting on news, good or bad, so he couldn't sleep. He spent the entire night watching Belle sleep while he thought of the worst scenario and planned.

And sure enough, after Doc had done an anal probe, examining, seeing the deteriorating walls of my brother's intestines on the screen as the probe extended into Amere's stomach, black spots covered the lining of Amere's stomach.

Amere looked at the screen while Doc retracted the probe. Doc silently went to the sink and began sterilizing his hands.

"Can I get dressed? Doc?"

"Yeah."

When Doc turned toward Amere, Amere saw the sadness and compassion in Doc's eyes.

"What's what?"

Doc admired my brother. Amere had been the wild one on line with Doc and Ellis Collins. Amere had helped Doc come out of his shell and helped financially to open Doc's clinic.

"Nupe, do I have colon cancer? Tell me!"

"Yes."

"We can cut it out, right?"

"This isn't my area of expertise."

"Is all that black shit on the screen cancer?"

"Yes. This is the lining of your stomach. Nupe, this much cancer has to be painful. Why did you wait so long to get checked out?"

"I don't know. What stage is it in?"

"The last."

"Before it goes away?"

"Before it destroys the lining of your stomach."

"Then what?"

"Get your affairs in order."

"Damn! ... We're all going to die one day, right, Nupe?"

Doc remained silent while fighting back tears.

Chapter 24
Interrogation

Since the students being interviewed could be potential suspects, most of their parents had brought along their lawyers, and were hesitant about their children deluging information. It was like Ellis Collins was pulling teeth, and the parents, children, and the lawyer were resisting.

"... I know you were at the skip party–"

"That doesn't mean she knows anything about drugs or an overdose." For most of the interviews, the lawyers did the speaking.

"I'm not saying she did or didn't, but I have two witnesses saying they asked everyone at the party to give the overdosed victim a ride to the hospital but that would be up to a jury to decide. I'm not trying to indict your child. I'm trying to protect your child and find the source of the drugs. Who was at the party giving away or selling ecstasy?"

The lawyer whispered to the parents, then the parents to their child, who whispered to the lawyer, who then became the mouthpiece.

"My client doesn't know a name."

"I'll be grateful for any information."

"This will exonerate my client from any charges?"

"Yes."

The student then freely answered,

"I don't know his name, but he's black and hangs out sometimes at the gym."

"Is he tall, a senior, or a freshman?"

"He's short and cute. But I don't think he attends school here. But I saw him give Lisa's boyfriend something."

"Who does he hang out with?"

"I've seen him talking with A.J. several times."

"Amere James Jr., the baseball player?"

"Yes, sir."

Several of the students interviewed knew the dark-skinned, short, cute guy, but didn't know his name or his whereabouts. What they did remember was that they had seen the guy with several jocks or just hanging with the in crowd,

"... Cheerleaders, the guys that play sports, and the rich kids."

"Just give me two names from the in-crowd you've seen him with."

"Jasmine and A.J."

Ellis Collins had the principal scheduled an interview with Amere, Belle, and Viola, who had arrived with two lawyers. A.J. and Jasmine were both trying to speak for themselves, furious about the whole idea of being interviewed,

"... I haven't missed any days."

"Why are we being interviewed?"

Amere and Ellis Collins were both strong-willed men who had respect and love for each other. But nothing came before Amere's family, not even the bond with his sands.

"Be quiet, Nupe. What's the purpose of this?"

"I'm trying to pinpoint the source of the ecstasy."

"What in the hell does this have to do with my children?"

Ellis Collins went into his explanation, but it was directed more at the children, "Several of the students who attended described the source but didn't know the name. But what they did remember was seeing the young, handsome, short black teenager hanging with A.J., and a couple of times seen flirting with Jasmine. By no means am I accusing you two of any wrongdoing. We've asked you here because I need your help before another person overdoses."

"What do you actually want from my children?"

"The youngster's name. ..." Ellis Collins saw the intensity in Amere's face. "... I asked Ebony the same question."

"You're muthafuckin' liar. You didn't ask your daughter to be an informant!"

Ellis Collins observed how the principal, the school's attorney and Amere's two lawyers were viewing the unorthodox style the interview had taken.

"Mr. James, can I speak with you in the hallway alone, please?"

Amere stood fast, only gritting at Ellis Collins. Amere knew the value of his children's reputation and how big a part it would play as they became a definite force in the world one day.

"... Sands, please?" Ellis Collins was pleading with my brother. Amere couldn't deny hearing Ellis Collins, so he followed him into the hallway.

"Sands, I put it on our bond and Melisa's grave that I asked Ebony. I want to get this murderer off the streets. He knows how lethal the strength of the pills he's slinging is."

"I want you to catch this bastard, but I'm not going to allow you to smear my children's reputation."

"You know it's on you if another person ODs, and they could've stopped it, but you didn't allow them."

"Muthafucka!"

"Sands one question–"

"Shut up! I know what I'm going to do. ..." Amere led the way back into the office, "... Ask your one question."

"Do either of you know a short, dark-skinned male who is handsome and well-dressed, and doesn't attend school here?"

Amere quickly intervened, "Wait, don't answer. Whatever your answer is, whisper it to me."

After both Jasmine and A.J. had spoken into their father's ear, Amere relayed, "That could be too many people."

"That could be selling ecstasy."

Both children shook their heads, meaning no.

"Could you each give me a list of your friends?"

"Hell naw! This interview is over! Let's go. If Melisa were alive, she would snap the shit out of you for asking Ebony for a list of her friends!"

Chapter 25
A Dangerous Favor

Jackson Wallace had replayed the time he was with Pearl over and over. What bothered him was his aggressiveness at the hotel, how it could harm him if she pressed the issue of rape. He left his office early.

The same overweight hotel clerk was on duty, and recognized Jackson Wallace as soon as he entered the lobby.

"How are you doing today, Mr. Wallace?"

"I'm fine, thank you. Seth?" Reading the name on the man's name tag.

"What can I do for you today, sir?"

"Seth. I'm here to do you a favor, because I need a man of your caliber on my team. Seth, how long have you worked here?"

"Six years, sir."

"If you don't mind, how much do you bring home a year?"

"With overtime, about 24."

"I have an open position for a survey director. Its starting salary is 32k a year, if you're interested."

"Yes, sir. Yes, sir, I'm interested. When can I start?"

Jackson Wallace leaned in closer to the man, "As soon as you give me all the surveillance footage for the date of March 16."

Jackson Wallace was in the office overlooking the gambling establishment. He hadn't told anyone about the incident with Pearl, but it was eating at him. It could cost him his dream.

Pho entered and studied Jackson Wallace, staring into nothing, with three discs in his hand.

"What's what?"

Jackson Wallace wasn't one for incriminating himself, but he had to get someone else's view of the matter.

"I think Pearl might cry rape."

"Did you?"

"Naw! But I was rough."

"You want me to handle her?"

"No. If something happens to her, her family will just escalate things. She might keep her mouth shut. How can she explain it to Devin?"

"What are those?"

"A precaution. Send Gigi up."

Chapter 26
Facing Reality

Pearl and my mother had a bond more like daughter and mother instead of mother-in-law to daughter–in-law. Pearl's mother had passed away when Pearl was in college. Her dad had remarried and retired to Miami for the warmer climate, so Pearl had gone to my mother for support and to confide in.

My mother had patiently and silently listened to Pearl's account of the rape, and then there were a few seconds of silence. My mother didn't judge; she just placed a hand on top of Pearl's, understanding the pain and conflict Pearl was dealing with.

"... I don't think Devin believes me."

My mother wasn't afraid to shine light in areas where Pearl or anyone else wanted to ignore.

"Why, baby?"

"Since Melody, he hasn't been willing to deal with reality. He doesn't understand me or hear me."

My mother knew I was seeing a therapist and how badly I was hurting over the loss of my angels.

"Well, if this doesn't snap him back to reality, nothing will. Are you going to allow this muthafucka that violated you to destroy your marriage, or are you going to prove to the world you were raped?"

"What about Devin?"

"That's something you've got to ask yourself."

Pearl started her own investigation at the scene of the crime, the hotel. A sympathetic female was on duty as the manager.

"The tapes are missing for that date. I'm sorry."

"Do tapes usually come up missing?"

"It's rare, but it happens. Someone might have mistakenly taped over it. I'm sorry."

Pearl was frustrated but was still clear-minded enough to think,

"Maybe I can speak with the desk clerk for that date."

"He quit."

"Can I have his contact information?"

"I'm not supposed to do this. You didn't get it from me."

"Thank you."

Once in the car, Pearl immediately called the number.

"... Is this Seph Owens?"

"Yes. Who is this?"

"This is Pearl James. I was wondering if we could meet and discuss the night of March 16th?"

"What about it?"

"I'll feel more comfortable discussing it face to face."

"Lady, I'm a busy man. What is this about, or I'm hanging up?"

"Do you remember seeing City Councilman Jackson Wallace–"

The line went dead, then when she redialed it, it went straight to voicemail over and over again. A conspiracy theory immediately started dancing in her head. She understood; anyone who thought highly of Jackson Wallace wouldn't help her cause.

It took Pearl two days to find the name of Jackson Wallace's ex-secretary.

Once she did, Pearl made friends with her on Facebook. She was a post-grad political science student at UAB and was happy to meet with Pearl, and even more so to testify as a character witness of Jackson Wallace's behavior.

"... This is a list of other women he's taken advantage of. I stole them when I realized his evil ass was about to let me go."

"Thank you. Thank you so much."

Over the next few weeks, Pearl met with a female elementary school teacher, a female evangelist, and a female public defender, all of whom felt as if they'd been raped, and all agreed to testify to it. With their testimony, Jackson Wallace's semen, and the test results of her blood work, Pearl believed she had a strong enough case to convict Jackson Wallace.

Chapter 27
Ecstasy

Sweep after sweep of the city's high schools hadn't gotten Ellis Collins any closer to finding the source. But the skip parties had stopped, and parents understood his actions.

Ellis Collins' appeals had been repeatedly broadcast on the local evening news shows,

"... There is an epidemic of overdoses among high school students. Somehow, the misconception of ecstasy pills being harmless and strictly a feel-good party enhancer is killing our children. Predators are preying on our children, making millions of dollars off of our children's consumption of this could be lethal and highly addictive drug! High school is not intended to cradle our children into the prison pipeline but is meant to be a pipeline to a career. We must safeguard our future. That is exactly what our children are. The quicker we can stop this predator, the safer our children will be. Thank you for your cooperation."

The parents saw Ellis Collins as being sincere and caring, the television news and the Birmingham newspaper saw him as a means of raising ratings and selling copies, doing official polls of the mayoral candidates, including Ellis Collins, who was only two percent behind Jackson Wallace, but ahead of the rest of the pack by 23 percent. The poll sparked more controversy, with reporters trying to question Ellis Collins whenever he exited or arrived at the police station.

"When will you officially announce your bid for mayor?"

"My interest is keeping our city safe." Ellis Collins would then drive off or walk off, leaving them with nothing absolute.

But Ellis Collins had told the truth; he was locked in on finding the source of ecstasy pills.

With the sweeps, several students had been caught with a few ecstasy pills in their lockers. They were users, not even petty hustlers, and mostly girls.

Instead of arresting them, Ellis Collins and the principal called the students' parents or guardians to the school. The sessions were private, one-on-one, so to speak. Ellis Collins' façade was stern, even though what he was saying had an undercoating of compassion.

"This is the first time your child has had a run-in with the law. ..." Ellis Collins picked up the bag of four pills, making sure the parents saw them. "Since your child is 16 years of age, this is a felony, which could be a punishment of six years. But the principal and I believe your child needs rehab instead of prison. But under two terms, your child has to fully cooperate in catching her supplier, then complete a rehab program."

All of the students agreed to the terms without any urging from their parents, giving Ellis Collins all the information they knew.

Ellis Collins had a nickname. "Chip," the suspect's cell number, and the color and make of the car the young man drove. But the cell was off and registered to a dead person. Ellis Collins ran into another dead end. He was at the station, reviewing all the students, from all the schools, who had been caught with the ecstasy pills, trying to find a connection between the students and the source, repeatedly writing a question mark until he heard a loud voice shouting.

"Goddamnit! I said I was raped! At least look at the muthafuckin' evidence I have in front of you!"

Ellis Collins stepped out of his cubicle to see a hysterical Pearl and a disinterested detective.

"Whoa. Whoa. I've got her. ..." Ellis Collins put an arm around Pearl's shoulder, calming her while leading her back to his cubicle.

"Did you say raped?"

"Yes! But everyone here is afraid to bring charges against Jackson Wallace!"

"City Councilman Jackson Wallace?"

"Yes! This is my affidavit and several other women's affidavits swearing they also were raped by Jackson Wallace. This is my medical report with the result of the blood test showing I was drugged, and they have the semen that was removed from me on record. If you can get him to submit to a DNA test, it will prove it's his semen."

"Does Devin know this?"

"Yes. He wanted to kill him, but now. ..." Pearl's expression finished the statement of uncertainty.

"I'm going to do a follow-up on this, and if it's concrete, I'll get the indictment."

Between beating the streets looking for a youngster named Chip that drove a black Camaro, Ellis Collins interviewed the women on Pearl's list. They were all beautiful, highly intelligent, and in their physical prime, 26 to 32, and extremely independent. They had been tricked, manipulated, lied to, deceived, but not physically raped. What was worse, they were still in love with Jackson Wallace, so they hated him.

Belle met Ellis Collins over lunch. It was her first time hearing that Pearl was raped and is pressing charges against Jackson Wallace.

"That's my sister-in-law, and I love her to death. I didn't know. I don't know why she hasn't told me."

"Was she drinking heavily that night?"

"No more than April and me."

"How long were you gone from the club?"

"Too long, if all this happened while I was gone."

"What mindset was Pearl in that night?"

"The same as mine and April's. We were there to feel good about ourselves, to enjoy the night, then go home."

"Does that mean going to a hotel with someone?"

"I don't believe Pearl will ever cheat on Devin!"

.....

April worked as the administrator of the Health Department, across the street from Doc's clinic. She walked over and joined Doc and Ellis Collins, happily showing off her engagement ring.

"Congratulations."

"Thank you. You're going to get that son-of-a-bitch?"

"That's what I'm trying to determine now. I have your medical reports, but I need to know if it was a forced penetration?"

"She's a married woman who delivered twins."

"Were there bruises?"

"Yes. On her shoulders."

"As if she'd been held down to submit?"

"No, more as if she was being supported, held up against her will."

"Doc, if you were called as a medical expert, could you testify that you have medical proof that Pearl was raped?"

Doc looked into April's eyes, then regrettably shook his head.

"No."

"Whose side are you two on? You know Pearl wouldn't cheat on Devin! Or lie about this!"

"I believe her, but I have to be able to prove it beyond a reasonable doubt."

.....

Ellis Collins was lying naked in bed with Annette. She was in his arms, but he was staring at the ceiling, thinking of Pearl and my relationship, of how it'd mirrored his and Melisa's devotion and love.

"Where are you?"

"Pearl accused Jackson Wallace of rape. I believe her, but there's no physical proof to even bring charges against him."

"Are you taking this case for Devin?" Annette knew how he thought.

"For both of them. Pearl wouldn't cheat on him, and she wouldn't lie. ..." Ellis Collins sat up, then gathered himself on the edge of the bed.

Annette didn't like the fact of his leaving her bed after they'd made love; he always had to go home to check on Ebony and his mother-in-law.

"Do you think Jackson Wallace is capable of rape?"

"I can't speak on clients."

"I'm not speaking from a professional aspect of dealing with him. I want your personal opinion of him."

"I don't know him personally. ... Stay until I fall asleep. Please?"

Chapter 28
Scandal

Jackson Wallace carried on like it was business as usual, literally being a middleman, connecting people and businesses, promoting job fairs and himself.

"... There's a pool of resources right here in Birmingham to attract big businesses. ..." During Jackson Wallace's speech, his cell had been vibrating the entire time.

Jackson Wallace finally answered once headed toward the limo. Jasmine was following behind him, reading his itinerary, "You still have–" He raised his hand, silencing her, listening to the voice of his friend, the DA, on his cell.

"You are being unofficially investigated for rape by Ellis."

As soon as the door of the limo closed behind Jasmine, Jackson Wallace exploded into the cell.

"That muthafuckin' bitch lying! I swear to God I didn't rape her!"

Jasmine knew the conversation was about her Aunt Pearl, so she intently listened.

" ... He has your semen. Is it yours?"

"More than likely. We fucked! It was consensual!"

"He's going to ask for you to submit to a DNA test."

Jackson Wallace pressed a button, and the driver let down the divider.

"Yes, sir?"

"Go by the headquarters. We're calling it a day." He ended his conversation on his cell, then stared at Jasmine. "Your aunt is a lying, evil bitch!"

Jasmine didn't know how to react. Her dad had taught her family first, but Jackson Wallace was the man she'd given herself to, so she remained silent.

Damage control was all Jackson Wallace could think of. Without any physical proof, he knew he wouldn't be charged, but his political career would be in jeopardy if he couldn't keep the damage under control. He couldn't seem weak or fragile in a time of crisis. He had to maintain a solid image, starting with the support of his wife. If she gave the pretense, others wouldn't have a choice but to accept his version.

Jackson Wallace's wife could tell he was troubled as soon as he entered their home.

"What's wrong?"

"How do you know?"

"You're home before ten." She wasn't naïve. She understood and admired his ambitions and dreams.

"I'm being investigated."

"I've told you to cut ties with him. He's served his purpose."

Jackson Wallace sat next to her, then slowly lowered the book from her face. She noticed the seriousness in his expression.

"What is it?" Once he lowered his head and looked away, she became angry, "What is it? You've gotten one of those whores pregnant?"

"No. No-ooo! They're investigating me for rape. I didn't do it! I didn't do it!" He had to hold her down to keep her from getting up.

"I don't give a shit! I told you. I told you! I want a divorce!" She was a politician's wife, but after decades of embarrassment from affairs, she was done. She'd warned him that if anything was to become public, she would leave him.

Jackson Wallace literally wouldn't release her,

"I know. I know. Just stay with me. I promise I'll get help. I'll go back to therapy. ..." Since their relationship had started as an arrangement, he appealed to the businesswoman in her.

"Just think about the kickbacks. I'll be a board member of every company that comes, once I'm mayor."

Even being furious at him, she couldn't fight back her tears.

"I'm pregnant! And you're throwing away our future because you can't keep your damn dick in your pants!"

She was like the others, she loved him. He'd charmed her and stolen her heart years ago; the only difference was that he had gained political clout by marrying her.

"I'm going to play your game, but you have to open a $4 million trust for the baby and me. That's $8 million. And you have to cut ties with him before he drags you into something else."

"Done. Get dressed."

"For what?"

"We're going out celebrating. We're having a baby!"

She knew it was just more damage control; them being seen happily out and about as the loving couple.

Jackson Wallace was sheepish when it came to the judge, but he had no choice in the matter. He had to tell his father. The judge had the real influence to put the right twist to dispel what would be considered only a rumor if no charges were ever brought forth.

The judge was disappointed in Jackson Wallace, but wasn't about to allow him to ruin their legacy so he held secret meetings with Rev and other prominent leaders in the city, who were all members of the same order. They concocted an anti-smear campaign.

"This will make you seen as the victim, and it'll dirty Ellis Collins' hands if he does decide to enter the race."

Jasmine showing up at Jackson Wallace's headquarters was a total surprise to him and his campaign manager, who were going over Jackson Wallace's speech.

Jackson Wallace stopped in the middle of a sentence.

"Give us a minute," pausing, then smiling at Jasmine while waiting as his campaign manager hesitated, "Give us a moment."

"We do have a speech to give."

"Give us a moment." Jackson Wallace closed the door behind him, then focused on Jasmine. "You believe in me?"

"I'm here."

"The rest of your family isn't."

"You have a speech to give." Not really wanting to think of her family, Jasmine led the way to the limo.

The campaign manager immediately started prepping Jackson Wallace, who was listening but more focused on Jasmine's body; the way the business skirt suit hugged her curves, her ample hips, the way her ass bubbled out, then the thickness of her calves.

At the limo, Jackson Wallace took the note cards from his campaign manager, then put a hand on the man's chest to stop him from entering.

"I can handle this. I'll call you later. Great job on the speech."

Jackson Wallace's smile was truly of self-confidence, but it was also an illusory reassurance to others that he was in control, which is how Jasmine felt as he stared at her.

"You understand things have changed. I mean, I can't stop the way I feel for you, but with your aunt's accusation, my wife will be close to me in public. My wanting to be mayor isn't about me. It's about helping the people in our city who can't help themselves. They need me to be mayor." Her hand touched his in a sign of support, and he leaned over, and his mouth covered hers. His hand caressed her breasts, then he sat back, knowing Jasmine was just as aroused.

"Damn, I want you right now," he said, acting as if hc couldn't control his desires,

"But we don't have time." Then started kissing her, but more intensely, before stopping again.

"You're going to have to help me relieve it."

Jackson Wallace started unfastening his belt and pants, then stopped once he noticed Jasmine was reaching under her skirt, about to remove her panties.

"We don't have time, but you can give him a kiss. Help me relieve the stress this way."

Jasmine understood his meaning, even though she'd never performed oral sex before. Her hair fell forward, covering her face as she took him into her mouth.

As the limo pulled into the parking structure of the Boutwell, Jackson Wallace was draining his essence into Jasmine's throat. When they stepped out of the limo, no one knew the difference. It was a press release, and Jackson Wallace's die-hards were there to support him along with every local news crew.

Jackson Wallace's wife met him at the podium, giving the appearance of if they were the happy couple.

"You've heard the accusations by now. I'm here today to set the record straight. The Lord and my wife have forgiven me for an extramarital affair that was totally consensual. The rest is a smear tactic by an aggressive detective that would like nothing better than to be the next mayor. ..."

Chapter 29
Divided Loyalties.

A rift had been created, dividing the city. The aftershocks had caused a hairline fracture to develop in my family.

A.J. and Jasmine had lunch at the same time. A.J. sat at the table, gritting his teeth, obviously mad.

"What's up with you?" Jasmine knew something was bothering her brother.

"What's up with you?"

"What do you mean?"

"Why're you turning your back on Aunt Pearl, still working with that sleazy ass dude? And why are you not answering any of Monte's calls?"

"Jackson Wallace isn't sleazy! And he's not a rapist! He's a good man! ... I love Aunt Pearl, but I overheard her and my mom talking about Uncle Devin's erectile dysfunctions and how horny she was." Jasmine was pissed, so much that she took her tray up without touching her food.

.....

With the publicity Jackson Wallace was getting from the testimonial speeches he was giving around the city, using a local hotel to sex Jasmine was out and Jasmine didn't feel comfortable sexing him in the limo just riding around town. So he drove her to his hideaway place on the lake.

Jasmine took it as a romantic getaway and allowed him to have sex with her anyway he wanted. She was in love, and that was what a woman did: pleased her man.

Jackson Wallace knew he was her first everything, and that was what got him off.

Jackson Wallace had worn himself out, and his snoring wouldn't allow Jasmine to sleep. She pretended it was their place as she walked around totally nude while fixing sandwiches.

She tried to wake him, but he was too exhausted to wake up to eat.

"I'll be ready to go in an hour. Wake me up then."

Jasmine sat back in bed, eating, then used the remote to turn on the television, but mistakenly hit the DVD play button to see the footage of Jackson Wallace semi-forcing or really helping Pearl out of the car and somewhat dragging her into the hotel, all the way to the room.

Jackson Wallace rolled over toward her, so she quickly turned it off. His snoring revealed he was still asleep. Her love for him made her see that her aunt was drunk and Jackson Wallace was supporting her.

Chapter 30
The Rally for Truth.

While some had backed away from Pearl, April was there for her, defending her when she heard a group of women gossiping at the fitness center.

"Y'all some messy bitches! I said it! No means muthafuckin' no! And since he wouldn't stop, he raped her!"

April bumped into the one who was talking as she passed on her way to the upper runner track, where Pearl was stretching.

April and Pearl were on their third lap when Belle finally joined them. Belle had been running by Pearl's side but silently. She'd sensed the change in Belle.

"I'm glad you could join us. I believe I'm going to have to publicly press the police department to get them to bring charges against Jackson Wallace."

"How?"

"Daily Strength and R.A.I.N.N. will come out and support me if I stage a public rally." Belle hadn't spoken, but her expression, the grimace on her face, said she didn't approve.

"What are you thinking, Belle?"

Belle stopped running, prompting April and Pearl to do the same.

"Please don't destroy this man's reputation because you're trying to save your marriage." Belle wasn't being hateful; her request was sincere.

"If you did the deed, you and Devin can work it out. The city needs Jackson Wallace as mayor." She was being brutally honest but her sensitivity could be felt in her tone.

"He drugged me and forced me into the hotel, then raped me! He's a two-faced monster! How can the people trust him?"

"Who else do they have?"

"I don't know but not him."

.....

Pearl was in her office at the recreation center when one of her sorority sisters, who was also a city counselor, entered. They were members of the same grad chapter.

Pearl had told her grad chapter two days earlier the predicament of her rape and the time and date of her press release and had asked for their support. The majority of her sorors had seemed sympathetic and supportive, promising they would be there. So, when the city councilor entered, Pearl was somewhat excited.

"I'm glad you stopped by. Tell me how my speech sounds–"

"Everyone knows how passionate you are about housing the needy. The position of superintendent of the housing authority is yours if you want it."

"What happened to Lois?"

"She's resigning, once you accept to replace her."

"She's okay with this?" The skepticism showed in Pearl's expression.

"Yes, she's running for representative of District 13."

It all started to fit together. District 13 was the district Jackson Wallace represented, plus Lois and Pearl had never been friends; honestly, they didn't like each other.

"What is this about?"

"Do you want the job?"

"Yes, I do."

110

"It's yours; all you have to do is drop your complaint and call off your rally."

"Get your ass the hell out of my office! Now!"

Chapter 31
Campaign Battles.

The judge's plan to buy Pearl's silence hadn't worked, but Jackson Wallace's speeches were just as powerful as Pearl's. Even with Pearl going public, Jackson Wallace had only dropped 5 percent in the polls. But the interim mayor also turned up her campaign, trying to gather all the sympathetic voters who believed Pearl.

"This state has lived through one monster named Wallace; let's not repeat the mistake." The interim mayor attacked Jackson Wallace in the hope of retaining her position.

Jackson Wallace's grassroots following showed their loyalty, coming out in full force to every event to show their support. And Jackson Wallace rallied their calling.

"... I have the ability to keep taxes low and regulations reasonable, as well as initiate incentive programs to lure businesses into our city to make employment soar in our city," Jackson Wallace was at his best in front of a crowd. "I have fought tooth and nail to pass city grants to lure employers. But as mayor, I will implement them myself!"

Jackson Wallace was doing as his campaign manager was advising, not speaking of the allegations but focusing strictly on jobs and issues that directly affected the people.

Still, the polls showed the interim mayor's rating climbing.

"She's not a threat. Stick to the script."

Jackson Wallace stayed disciplined on the campaign trail.

"I focus on long-term solutions, such as ending a heroin-like addiction to welfare that many people have. Meeting our challenges will require serious solutions, but above all, it will require serious leadership a quality in high demand in our city, and among my opponents on this campaign trail."

Since Jackson Wallace led the pack in the polls, he was the target of all the would-be Mayors.

"He speaks of ending a heroin-like addiction to welfare, but at the same time would give city grants, your hard-earned taxpaying dollars, to companies with little say in how they spend it. I call that corporate welfare, which is four times more costly–"

Jackson Wallace turned off the television in the office of his campaign headquarters and then turned to his campaign manager.

"This bitch doesn't know how stupid her ass really is. I'm not concerned with her. I want to counteract him." He held up the newspaper, which had a picture of Ellis Collins in front of a high school.

"Sources say he's not going to enter."

The same newspaper had held an unofficial straw poll that had Ellis Collins 4 percent above Jackson Wallace.

"What source? I don't leave shit to chance! Don't worry. I'll handle it." Jackson Wallace turned the television back on.

The news was showing a clip of Ellis Collins addressing a crowd of adults in front of a high school.

"... Overdoses among students are increasing. Nearly one in eight high school students admits to using illegal drugs. Ecstasy's popularity is growing as a recreational drug. This is the wrong message being sent to our children!"

Jackson Wallace went back into his bag of tricks he'd used as a DA; he'd gotten the locations of local high-profile drug houses from his partner. Jackson Wallace personally called all the local news stations, then once the news teams arrived at the site, Jackson Wallace, along with a team of his police friends, drove a bulldozer through the house until it was completely leveled.

"... This's my city! You will not be selling poison in it on my watch!"

Jackson Wallace didn't stop there; he went on sting operations where the corner stores were selling tobacco and liquor to minors. He took full advantage of the free publicity, and his ratings grew in the polls; in the straw poll, his rating even surpassed Ellis Collins.

Chapter 32
Last Wish.

The realization of death had settled in with my brother. He was getting his affairs in order.

Amere sat at the kitchen table of Viola's, waiting. She entered from a day's work, then sized him up, the contentment in his smile. He seemed pleased at peace.

"What's what?"

"I have something for you." He held up a travel brochure and extended it to her.

"Check your savings account when you get a chance."

Viola started screaming when she saw the destinations ranging all over the world on the itinerary.

Tears ran from her eyes as she sat in his lap.

"I'll always love you, Babe. ..." She saw how he was grimacing, in obvious pain. "...What's wrong?"

"Me, it has always been me. I'm so sorry for the years of pain I've caused you. You deserve better."

Viola's joy was slowly fading,

"What do you mean?"

"I put two million in your account. I want you to enjoy life, meet someone deserving of you, and fall madly in love."

"No. Noooo! You're not leaving me after all these years. I love you, and you love me. You just said it. We can leave things the way they are." She began to openly cry.

Amere wiped away her tears. "I'm dying. I want to do right by you and Belle before it happens."

"So, you're just leaving me?"

"You should've left me years ago, but now I'm doing you a favor, so you can have the happiness you deserve."

Viola allowed him to get up, then shed tears as she watched him leave.

Chapter 33
More Allegations.

Ellis Collins had hit a wall with both investigations, even though the captain had officially given him orders to investigate the rape and to have a detailed report on his desk ASAP. The publicity of Pearl's speeches was gaining support and applying pressure, plus the acting mayor's campaign needed help. The order gave Ellis Collins an extended grace period to continue using his unit to sweep the high schools.

Ellis Collins had scheduled an appointment to meet with Jackson Wallace. The two had worked on several cases together. He knew Jackson Wallace wasn't beyond stepping into the gray area. Ellis Collins had seen him go there several times to get a monster off the streets when the case wasn't as solid as Jackson Wallace had manipulated the jury to believe.

Jackson Wallace was in the office of his campaign headquarters, along with Jasmine, whom Ellis Collins was somewhat surprised was still working with the campaign.

"Good evening." Ellis Collins paused, waiting for acknowledgement from the two of them.

"Good evening. Ms. James, will you update the Twitter account with these, please?"

"Good evening." Jasmine answered Ellis Collins' stare as she left the office.

The arrogance of Jackson Wallace's tone drew Ellis Collins' attention from the closing door.

"Detective Collins, this is the jest of the evening your investigating; Mrs. James and I had drinks and danced at the club. We flirted a little while, then I offered to take her home. Our flirting led us to mess around in the car, which ended in a hotel bed. After we'd done the deed and were lying in the aftermath, Mrs. James' guilt must have gotten the best of her because her entire attitude changed. She became irate, so I left her there. The entire encounter was consensual."

"Can you explain the bruises on her shoulders?"

"I know nothing of any bruises. Wait, she was tipsy and almost fell when we were leaving the club. I caught her."

"Can I have a swab of the inside of your mouth for DNA reference?"

"There's no need. The semen is mine."

"Were you and Mrs. James having an affair?"

Jackson Wallace couldn't help but laugh. He could see that his conceitedness irked Ellis Collins, and he knew his answer would surely make him angrier. "No, she was a one-night stand."

Ellis Collins' cell kept buzzing; it was a good distraction from the nonsense Jackson Wallace was speaking, at least until Ellis Collins read the text, giving him the directions to another OD'd student.

"I'm sorry. We're going to have to continue this interview at a later date."

"I would think you would close this case with the lack of evidence."

"I'm investigating a complaint to see if there is enough evidence for an indictment."

"Surely you're done with the investigation."

"No, I'm not sure. I'll contact you if I need your answer to any more questions."

The body of the OD'd girl wasn't far from the campaign headquarters, less than three blocks, across from a McDonald's.

The coroner was already there, with the body on a stretcher. Ellis Collins allowed the officer to continue questioning the boy and girl, who were overwhelmed by the loss of their friend.

"... She was always goofy, having fun. We thought she was goofing off until she stopped moving."

"Did you see her take any type of pills?"

"No. All she had was a milkshake."

"She did complain about having a headache, but I thought she was talking about a brain freeze."

"How long were you with her?"

"We meet at McDonald's every day before we go to work."

"She takes the bus from Ramsey."

"Where do you work?"

"We don't get paid. We volunteer at Jackson Wallace's campaign headquarters."

"Thank you for your cooperation. If we have any more questions, we'll contact you."

Through interviews of the girl's family and friends, Ellis Collins learned that she was another beloved, talented, promising, fearless, future leader, who loved life and that no one knew she was taking ecstasy pills. More frustration.

Back in his cubicle, Ellis Collins pinned a picture of the girl on the board next to the other OD'd students, then just stared, mentally trying to find the connection. Over the next few days, Ellis Collins tirelessly interviewed the family and friends of all the victims. The only connection other than several being schoolmates was that three out of the 12 volunteered at Jackson Wallace's campaign headquarters.

Whatever had a slim possibility, Ellis Collins checked into it. The stern stares of the females at the campaign headquarters didn't intimidate Ellis Collins. They assumed he was back investigating Pearl's claim there to destroy their hero. They all eyed him as he approached a young girl who immediately sounded her loyalty to Jackson Wallace,

"No, he has never made advances toward me!"

Ellis Collins gave her a second look. She was pretty but obviously still a minor.

"That's a good thing for his sake. But I'm not here for that. Do you know a short, handsome young black male named Chip who drives a black Camaro?"

The girl yelled across the room, "Chip! Come here!"

Ellis Collins turned in the direction she was speaking to see the back of a youngster running, headed for the door. Ellis Collins was in excellent shape and instantly chased after him.

People were getting off work, so the sidewalks were crowded, and cars were pulling out of the parking structures.

Chip had one thing on his mind: getting away from Ellis Collins. Shoving people out of his way wasn't a problem, but when Chip looked back to see if Ellis Collins was still coming, he ran into the side of a car exiting a parking structure.

Chip came to be handcuffed to a hospital bed with Ellis Collins standing over him. Ellis Collins had Googled Chip while he lay unconscious, finding out that he was an honor roll student at Ramsey High School, was the school treasurer, and had already been accepted to the University of Alabama.

What was impressive on Chip's behalf was that he was from the Cottageville projects.

"You're going to wish you'd died. You are under arrest for 17 counts of murder and the distribution of a prohibited substance..." Ellis Collins realized Chip was smart enough to orchestrate the skip parties and even to have a network to move the pills at other high schools, but he doubted whether Chip was the mastermind behind the manufacturing of the pills. "You're looking at the electric chair."

"What if I give up everybody that works for me?"

"I want who you work for."

"I can't."

"Then fry." Ellis Collins moved toward the door.

"Wait! Even if I give him to you, you won't be able to get him."

"Why?"

"Because he's protected."

"By whom?"

"Jackson Wallace!"

Ellis Collins silently re-evaluated the youngster; maybe he was the mastermind.

"Who do you work for?"

"Pho."

The name had been given hundreds of times, but the person was a ghost.

All anyone knew was the name Pho. No location, no solid description.

"Why are you trying me, youngster?"

"Pho is my oldest brother."

Ellis Collins knew he had something solid.

"Why would Jackson Wallace protect him?"

"They're partners. Have been since the fifth grade."

Chapter 34
F.O.E.

I'm far from a punk, so it was extremely hard for me not to beat Jackson Wallace to death with my bare hands when he entered my store, but I'd promised Pearl I would let the police handle it.

Jackson Wallace had a shit eating smirk while at the same time trying to explain his actions in a self-righteous manner. "... My involvement with your wife–"

Both of my girls immediately ran from the back of the store to my sides, screaming, drowning him out.

"Daddy, don't you believe him!"

"He's telling stories on mommy!"

I snapped, damn near reached over the counter, but Jackson Wallace quickly stepped back to his two bodyguards.

"You'd better pray you get found guilty because if not, you will get found dead! Get the fuck out of my store!" I didn't know if I was mad because he'd tried me as a man or if I believed he'd violated my wife.

I picked up my youngest daughter, consoling her while making sure Jackson Wallace left my store.

Ivy was crying into my neck, "Daddy, do you love Mommy? Daddy, do you love Mommy?"

Chapter 35
Blood.

A fight pit was located between Birmingham and Leeds. Amere was there gambling on the street fighters, while waiting on Coop and his team to arrive.

Pho and a crew of about eight street fighters were in the crowd, not far from Amere. Pho purposely started talking loudly to get Amere's attention. "That bitch ass hoe, Pearl James trying to fuck off Jackson's chance at being mayor! The hoe gave the pussy up. Even her punk ass husband knows it. What kind of man would let a muthafucka continue to breathe that raped his wife?"

Amere didn't care that he was only one unarmed man, or the fact that a solid punch to his stomach could rip his already thin lining.

"Yo muthafucka, you're talking about my brother and my sister-in-law! It would be wise of you to shut the fuck up!"

Pho's crew raised up as if to approach Amere, but froze once Coop and Amere's street fighters made their presence known.

Pho was a killer, but not to the same degree as Coop, and knew if it started, Coop wouldn't stop until all of them were dead, so Pho tried to settle his crew.

Amere wouldn't let it die. "Naw bitch made muthafucka, don't cry deuces now. Time to turn muthafucka. Bitch! Hoe! Get your bitch ass in the pit! Me and you!"

Pho recognized Amere as a businessman, a playa, a gambler but not as a killer, which Amere wasn't but he knew my brother could turn with the best.

All of that was transpiring between events and had become the event. The pit was empty when my brother stepped into it, still taunting Pho and his crew.

"Y'all following this bitch ass punk! Y'all must be some bitch ass punks, too!"

Amere wanted to embarrass Pho into getting into the pit. But Pho was a patient, smart killer, not a street fighter and just laughed.

Amere snatched the briefcase from Coop, then dumped it in the pit, a hundred grand in cash.

"Whatever you've got in your pocket! Which one of you bitches got the balls?"

Three out of Pho's crew immediately stepped up to the challenge. They were the best fighters out of Pho's crew. The bouts were intense. Every blow had the strength of a kill shot. Amere took some, but his hand speed and power proved too much. He punished each of them, one after the other, while taking side bets between bouts, talking trash, and taunting Pho.

"Get that up off him. Leave him in his boxers."

My brother had boxed since he was 10 years old, had been a Golden Glove champ, but was disqualified from going to the Olympics for gambling on his own fights. He always bet on himself.

"Ten to one odds. Put it on the wood."

After my brother had finally put the third fighter to sleep, Coop stepped in. My brother wasn't showing his pain, but Coop knew of his cancer and could tell by Amere's grimace that he was hurt.

"If anyone else wants to see him, you've got to deal with me."

Instead of going to the hospital like Coop wanted to take him, my brother came straight to my store pissed at me. He wasn't concerned about himself.

"How the fuck you gonna let this muthafucka get away with this shit!"

The reason I hadn't discussed it with him was that I knew how he would react. I just gritted my teeth at him, focusing on his bruised face and the dried blood in the corner of his mouth.

My silence infuriated him more, "You don't believe she was raped? Goddamnit! She wouldn't cheat on you! Why haven't you dealt with this muthafucka?"

Amere had started staring at me as if I were a coward, which took me over the edge.

"She made me promise to allow the law to handle it!"

"Fuck it! I'm dying. I'll do it!"

All that registered was that my brother was dying. It was as if I couldn't breathe.

"What?"

"I'll do it!"

"Not that. The dying part?"

"I've got cancer." Amere leaned against the counter as if the weight of saying it was extra heavy. "She wouldn't cheat on you."

My mind wasn't ready to accept the loss of another loved one. I heard, but I didn't hear my brother explaining how he wanted me to be Jasmine and A.J.'s financial guardian until they were 25.

Chapter 36
Decisions of The Heart.

Jackson Wallace had spent most of the morning and afternoon meeting with CEOs of Fortune 500 companies, "Support me, and I will welcome your plant in my city. There will be no city tax, and I'll petition the state to waive theirs, plus regulations will be eased …."

Jackson Wallace was negotiating deals that couldn't be refused. A win-win for both parties. Three companies issued press releases detailing their plans to begin building new factories in Birmingham and personally giving credit to Jackson Wallace for being a deciding factor, boosting his standing in the polls by double digits.

By the time Jasmine arrived that evening, Jackson Wallace was ready to celebrate; closing the office door behind her, he tried to bend Jasmine over his desk. Her resistance surprised him.

"What's wrong?"

"My period hasn't come."

Jackson Wallace went from joyful to concerned to upset, then calmed himself, "I used condoms."

Jasmine understood what he was insinuating and became pissed.

"You're the only person I've ever been with! Did the condom break?"

Jackson Wallace's expression showed he remembered it breaking.

"Yes. But we can't have it. Having it out of wedlock would smear me, and you, and my dreams and my dreams for you. We have to have an abortion."

The innocence showed on Jasmine's face, her sorrow somewhat mixed with wanting to understand.

Chapter 37
Bingo.

The weight of Pearl's public speeches wasn't only pressing the police department, but me as a husband. I wanted to crawl into my world, my comfort zone, something that would make me forget about the drama. Luckily, I'd scheduled a charity BINGO at the armory.

The questions from my girls stopped, they loved playing Bingo with their grandmother. So, while the noise from the event pleasantly drowned out my own questions that had been screaming around in my head. Every table was packed with people and cards. Each card was a $5 donation. The prizes were 3D televisions and iPhones, which had been donated. No one stared at me with wondering eyes. They were focused on their cards, concerned with their numbers.

I'd relieved the card girl who was accepting the donation for the cards. Before I could take a seat, Annette and Hazel stepped to the window. Hazel and I had dated in high school, but she was a year older than I was, and couldn't stand Birmingham more than she loved me. She was still beautiful. Annette took the cards, then realized Hazel was stuck smiling at me. It was the first time we'd seen each other in 28 years.

"I'm going to find a place to sit."

"I'll be there in a moment," which turned out to be never.

Hazel and I talked of our past, her stardom; her voice and talent, along with her beauty, had reached mega heights. Movies, stage plays, and CDs. She discussed the death of her husband and the fact that she regretted not having children. Hazel represented a time in my life when I didn't know pain.

"You know, they kept me updated on you. I figured you would be running for mayor."

"I would've if Melody's accident hadn't happened." I was the people's defender, but I couldn't save my children or my wife, or now my brother.

"I would love to meet your wife and children."

"I can arrange that. How long are you here for?"

"It's undetermined as of yet."

Chapter 38
Betrayal.

Jackson Wallace was spending time at the police station with his friends, the DA, and two detectives, really checking up on Ellis Collins, when he learned of the raid being planned on Pho's warehouse, where supposedly a manufacturing lab for ecstasy pills existed. He listened to their laughter, clowning Ellis Collins for chasing ghosts.

"It might not be so crazy. Keep me updated. I'll see you all tomorrow."

By the time Jackson Wallace was in his car, Pho was on his cell, listening to Jackson Wallace's demand,

"Meet me at the drug store."

The warehouse was designed like a meat freezer so the heat of manufacturing the drugs would be undetectable by any infrared thermal imaging. The lab was deserted, but Pho was there, somewhat pissed for being called away.

"What's this about?"

"They know about this place. They're on to you."

"They've been on to me for years. Doesn't anyone know about this place?"

"They're planning a raid in three days. They believe that's when you start production again."

The detailed information made Pho become serious.

"We're in this together, always have been. We can burn this muthafucka to the ground and build another somewhere else tomorrow."

"We don't need the drug money anymore."

Pho had already started throwing acid over everything.

"Like hell! Your campaign has eaten over half of the monthly profits since you're so fascinated with being mayor, with the kickbacks and a salary that doesn't compare with the ends we're making."

Pho turned to see Jackson Wallace with a gun pointed at him.

"... What! Are you gonna kill me or cover for me? Man, put that shit up. You're a politician. You ain't got the heart to pull that trigger."

Pho went to continue pouring the acid when two shots surprised him. He just stood there, staring in disbelief.

"You're right, this is strictly political. Nothing personal."

Pho fell dead, then Jackson Wallace had to drag the body to the barrel of acid and stuff him inside.

Jackson Wallace could see the smoke rising in his rear-view mirror as he drove off.

Chapter 39
Unspoken.

Hazel had volunteered to host my fashion show, which really elevated it to the event of the spring. She was spending more time at the store with me. I felt relaxed around her. At home, things were tense. I'd been sleeping in Ivy's room. The distance between Pearl and me was affecting Ivy the most.

I was reading to Ivy her favorite story when Pearl built up the courage to enter the room.

She was taking control determined to talk our problems out.

"I did go to the club looking for affection and attention, but not a lover. He raped me. He raped me!"

I couldn't move. The situation was too complicated for my mind to handle, to process.

Pearl stood there holding herself, crying. My daughters left me in the bed, and went to comfort their mother, tried to hug her, but Pearl only felt a chill. She started shivering while still crying, then just ran out of the room.

My daughters pleaded with me.

"Go after her!"

"Daddy, don't you love her?"

I didn't know. I didn't know if I wanted to go forward or back to a time when there was no pain in my life.

Chapter 40
The Facts.

Doc had arranged for two specialists to see Amere. It was somewhat heartbreaking when their diagnosis were the same as Doc's.

Amere swallowed the news as he'd been in a close fight, and had been out-punched but wanted to continue to fight, while knowing the bell was about to ring, ending it all. He didn't say anything, but Doc read his expression, knew his pain.

Doc stayed by Amere's side after the other doctors had left.

My brother shook it off with a smirk,

"I'm living now, so I ought to be happy now."

Tears fell from Doc's eyes as he smiled at the thought.

"You're right."

.....

Amere was at home and dressed, waiting to go to marriage counseling when Belle and Jasmine arrived moments apart. Belle stared at the bottle of XO that was in front of him on the table, along with the glass he was drinking from.

"We are going to be inside a church." Belle reached for the glass to have Amere move it.

"Are you ready to go?"

"I'm not wearing slacks to church."

"Well, go get dressed. Where are you in a hurry to?" Amere, staring at Jasmine who kissed his cheek, then was quickly walking off.

Jasmine stopped half of the way down the hallway, "I've got to change before I go to work. You told me not to wear my uniform."

"Hell naw! You're not still working for that rapist!"

"The police haven't arrested him, and he hasn't been found guilty."

"He raped your damn aunt! You don't work there anymore! You hear me?"

"Mom!"

"Call your damn mom. Call whoever the hell you like, but you better not take your ass back down to that headquarters!" He gritted his teeth at Belle, who'd stepped out into the hallway while getting dressed.

"I don't work there, but I'm voting for him." Belle put in her two cents, then returned to the room.

"Shittin' me! The hell if you do."

Belle's shouts echoed through the house. "Just how are you going to tell me who I can vote for?"

"I just did. C'mon, let's go before I change my mind. You'd better pray I don't go kill his ass."

Preston had a PhD in psychology. He was qualified to be a couples therapist, plus he was an ordained minister. Amere and Belle were in his office in the back part of AME. They'd been listening to his lecture-slash-sermon for almost 35 minutes nonstop.

"these shields do their job quite successfully; they keep us functioning and protected. They defend us from emotional and spiritual bruises so that we can carry on in our daily lives. ..."

Preston noticed Amere was somewhat bored, not really paying attention, while Belle was all smiles and nodding as she tightly held Amere's hand.

"Yet there are times when these defenses outlive their welcome, become obstacles preventing you from getting to the emotional high ground by undermining your long-term self-interest. These defenses have hardened into patterns of self-destructive or counterproductive behavior that you repeat over and over again. You have to know when you have done enough and have had enough–"

"Man, are you trying to help us or break us up?"

"You have spiritually bruised this woman for years, have patience. Have you given up on God's plan?"

"Man, fuck hell and Heaven. I've had enough of both of them. I love you, but if you want a divorce fine! I'm going home, if you're riding with me."

My brother left the office, but when Belle stood, Preston grabbed her hand.

"You deserve better. I love you. I'll leave my wife if you leave him." Preston pleaded, refusing to release her.

Belle snatched away from him.

"You were trying to break us up!"

The car ride home was in complete silence, not even the radio played. My brother was tired. It had been a long day for him.

Once inside their home, he tried to take a nap, but as soon as he was asleep, Belle felt affectionate. She was leaning in to kiss him. Out of natural reflex, his hand went up to shield his face, but the palm of his hand hit her directly in the mouth. He immediately felt the blood dripping on his chest from Belle's mouth.

The blood was actually pouring from between Belle's fingers as she held her mouth.

"You knocked out my muthafuckin' tooth!"

To see the blood and pain coming from Belle scared my brother.

"I–I, I didn't mean to. I was just covering up. We've got to get you to the hospital. C'mon."

Then he realized Belle was only in her bra and panties.

A house robe and pajamas were what Amere and Belle wore to the emergency room. The blood-soaked cloth Belle had to her mouth drew people's attention.

A suspicious female doctor examined Belle. The doctor was caring and gentle, but kept cutting her eyes at Amere.

"Was the tooth already loose?"

Belle knew the undertone of the question and was pissed at my brother but kept cool.

"Can you put it back in?"

"As soon as the swelling goes down. I know a cosmetic surgeon who can implant a tooth there and have you looking beautiful again. It doesn't require stitches. I'll be back in a moment."

Once the doctor left the room, Amere held Belle. She was furious, but unable to keep the tears from flowing. He knew she wanted to explode on him.

"I'm sorry, I'm so sorry. Maybe you can get that boob job and liposuction you wanted. I do love you, and I'm not just saying it."

The doctor reentered with a police officer.

"Mrs. James, Officer Williams has some questions he has to ask."

Instead, Amere asked them a question.

"What the hell is this about?"

"Sir, will you wait out in the hall, please?"

"Hell naw! Ask your question."

"Mrs. James, how did you get injured?"

"It was an accident."

"What kind of accident knocks out your tooth while you're in bed?"

Amere had had enough.

"Use your imagination! She said it was an accident. Doctor, can we have the information, please?"

The doctor reluctantly handed the card and prescription to Belle instead of my brother then both the doctor and policeman watched disappointedly as Belle left behind my brother.

Chapter 41
I Can See.

The turnout for the fashion show was phenomenal. The mall was packed.

Hazel and my mother had arranged the entertainment perfectly, and I'd enjoyed MC'ing the runway. The models strutted like the stars they were. Hazel's voice mesmerized the crowd.

Pearl hadn't been to the mall since Melody's accident, so I was totally surprised, but extremely happy when she came over to my mother, me, and Hazel.

"This was the best show so far. You all did great."

Unconsciously, I embraced my wife with a kiss and kept her in my arms.

"This is my wife, Pearl. This is Hazel." Both seemed impressed by the other. I saw Tiny Tots had so many people in it that I couldn't see the counter.

Melody and Ivy came to me.

"They can use some help with the customers."

My mother and I both headed off to the store, leaving Pearl along with Hazel.

"I can see why Devin loves you. I have to be honest with you. I've had a wonderful life, but many times I've wondered how it would've turned out if I'd chosen Devin instead of music."

It stunned Pearl; Hazel had said it so politely and friendly in a manner like it was a don't-worry-about-it. But didn't allow Pearl to respond.

"The store is extremely crowded. Maybe we should go help?"

Pearl walked with Hazel to the entrance, then backed away, looking as if she'd seen ghosts. Hazel entered anyway and immediately started helping customers.

The crowd in the mall didn't die down until closing time. My daughters and I were in the back, bringing out boxes to restock the racks and shelves.

Business had been so good; the store was close to empty, it looked as if it was going out of business. Everyone had left except Hazel, who sat at the counter, smiling at me.

"You don't have to ruin your night staying with me."

"You don't think I know that?" Hazel's movement was so sensuous as she came over and began helping to stock the racks.

"Introduce me to your daughters, please? I can sense them, but I can't see them."

Hazel had always been special, superstitious, and open about the supernatural, but her request had surprised me. I hadn't told her my daughters were dead.

My daughters started bugging me to introduce them.

"My little one is Ivy, and the one the size of her mother is Melody."

Hazel hugged them both, knowing that they both were embracing her.

"They both want to be a lawyer and a movie star and help house the poor like their mom."

"Your girls want to be like both of their parents." Hazel seemed sincere, not just putting on a show to be sensitive to me.

Chapter 42
The Art of Factoring.

My brother kidnapped me from the store the next morning. He was determined to teach me his method of making money work instead of working for money.

Out of all the properties he owned and leased, and his manufacturing businesses, factoring was what brought the most income each month. I knew the fundamentals of factoring, but Amere broke it down to its simplest form. He actually took me to Walmart and showed me the product of the company that we were about to meet with. It was a protein bar, a gourmet snack.

"Everyone wants to get their product in Wal-Mart, because they have so many stores, not realizing once they sign the deal, it's a trap. But at least we know Wal-Mart and the government will pay."

Factoring was like loan sharking, but legal. My brother sought out small companies with exclusive contracts with Wal-Mart and the government. These companies had the demand but had been tricked because Wal-Mart had an entire quarter to pay, but could reorder as many times in that quarter as needed.

The company was a nice-sized warehouse bakery with about 35 employees. Mostly everything was automated.

After the tour of the factory, the owner, who was also the CEO, took us to his office. He was a proud man who knew Wal-Mart had him by the balls.

"They're trying to restock their entire damn chain twice every quarter. They're bleeding me dry. They're trying to make me sell my company to them."

It was an interview, but Amere didn't interview people; he allowed them to talk while he evaluated them.

"My contract is up in two quarters. My books are in order. I need the cash to meet their demands so my company can survive until the contract expires."

"Why don't you just sell?"

The owner's face tightened, his hands became fists, and his defensiveness sounded in his tone.

"Not yet! Not yet. My product is only the first item of my brand. My brand will be the Hershey of healthy gourmet snacks, worth billions, then I'll think about selling."

I could tell my brother was going to make the loan; they had that think-big attitude, plus the loan was a win-win for my brother. He couldn't lose money by buying the payment accounts due with Wal-Mart being the one paying. He'd only have to wait 90 days for a 30 percent profit return for every dollar loaned.

Chapter 43
A Heartfelt Warning.

The shine of Jackson Wallace was fading to Jasmine, even though she was disoriented, but she still had him on a pedestal. She'd confided in Angel about her pregnancy.

"He's some shit!"

"You don't know what you're talking about."

"He's a piece of shit for spitting that weak ass shit at you."

"Shut up. It's best for both of us."

"He's still some shit."

"Bye. I've got to go."

Jasmine left Angel's home mad, but mostly angry with herself.

Jackson Wallace had stopped returning Jasmine's calls, and her dad would've killed her if he had heard she'd gone down to the campaign headquarters. But Amere hadn't said she couldn't attend any of Jackson Wallace's rallies.

Jasmine arrived to see Jackson Wallace walking through the crowd, shaking hands, kissing cheeks, and babies. Jasmine knew the route he was taking would lead to the limo. She was there waiting.

Once Jackson Wallace spotted Jasmine, he faked a pleasant smile and whispered, "Hey, beautiful..." As he hugged her, "... I've only got a moment. A meeting I can't miss."

Jasmine could tell she was getting brushed aside. "The appointment is next week."

"I'll be there right by your side. I promise. I've got to go. Bye beautiful. I'll see you."

Jasmine watched the limo drive off, then turned to leave to be face-to-face with Jackson Wallace's wife.

"Stay away from him. It's for your own good. He's Satan and has destroyed too many young girls' lives that were just as bright and ambitious as yours."

Jackson Wallace's wife wasn't threatening; it was a heartfelt warning that left Jasmine speechless before Jackson Wallace's wife walked off.

Chapter 44
I Don't Know.

I was at my session with Annette, lying on her couch, discussing what I was feeling toward Hazel, "… She understands I'm not crazy. She wants to talk about my daughters." I knew it without me saying. I didn't know what I felt for Hazel. I was just feeling good, enjoying talking about my angels. The time distracted me from the problems in my marriage.

"Pearl doesn't get this. She's not in tune with me anymore."

"Couples usually go in and out of emotional sync with each other during the course of their marriage. Invite Pearl to join us next week."

My hour was up. I'd arrived at the session feeling good, but as it ended, I was confused and didn't know how I felt about anything.

.....

Ellis Collins had scheduled a meeting with Pearl to relay the results of his investigation.

"I believe you were raped, but without physical evidence, I can't prove it without a reasonable doubt. But I'm not closing the case."

Pearl stayed strong until she got into the car, then broke down, beating the steering wheel, crying in anger.

I arrived home a little after eleven. Pearl was in the foyer staring at the doorway as I walked in. I could tell she'd been crying and was upset. I didn't know what to say or if she wanted me to say anything.

Her words stopped me from walking by her.

"I can smell her perfume on you. Are you sleeping with her?"

"Noooo!"

"Why are you spending so much time with her?"

"I just enjoy talking with her. She understands the girls."

My girls came out of their rooms, looking scared and tearful. They could see their mother becoming highly emotional.

"How does she understand? They came out of me! They were my babies! I'm the one you should be confiding in!"

"I can't! You don't want to talk about them! You want to act like they don't exist!"

"They don't! Not anymore!"

"They do! I can see them! I can hear them!"

"That's in your head! We have to deal with reality."

Pearl walked off from me, passing through my girls.

"Daddy, why can't mommy see us or feel us like Aunt Hazel?"

"Dad, is Mom going to leave?"

I didn't know the answers.

Chapter 45
Spring Break.

Spring break had started. Amere had both A.J. and Jasmine. They both knew something was physically wrong with their father, but not to what degree. They were riding over the city, checking on his businesses and properties, while he somewhat preached.

"I've had this idea dancing around in my head for several years. I want you and your brother to join forces and start a business."

Neither one of his children responded. They were both like their grandmother, who could squeeze the most out of a dollar.

"Let me rephrase it. I'm going to give you $500,000. I want you to start a business with it. Think long term."

"I'm going to be a politician."

"Who will respect a politician who can't make a profit in her personal life? They won't have the confidence you'll be able to run a city, a state, or a country if you can't run a business."

"What kind of business do you want us to start?"

"What's wrong with you? Both of y'all are intelligent. Use your imagination. Think big! Then make big things happen!" That was my brother's philosophy.

"It's all about entrepreneurs who can deliver choice, convenience, and influence aspects of people's lives."

"We can franchise a Nike Town, plus design our own Nike shoes and clothes!" A.J. had become excited, while Jasmine was skeptical.

"Can we invest it or buy properties something safe? So, if the economy doesn't turn around, we won't lose every penny?" Jasmine was thinking of safety.

"Stop being scared! You don't get it, it's very hard to fail completely. It might take a decade to become successful, but if you've got the big idea, all you need to be is prepared, stay persistent, and be patient, you'll succeed. Understanding this is important."

Amere's cell started to sing. It was Coop.

"How much? … As soon as I drop them off …. All right, I'm on my way."

"If that's Coop, tell him to bring Lucky." Jasmine loved her dog, but Belle wouldn't have dogs living inside the house.

"He heard you."

Amere pulled up to the fight pit in the back woods of Leeds,

"… respect boundaries with the threat of death, but corporate muthafuckas are more ruthless. Because there's no fear factor, they will cheat, lie, and steal with no regard or second thought of you. That's why you have to be prepared with knowledge and counseling of the situations."

Coop came to the car with Lucky, a runt of a white pit bull. Jasmine opened the back door, and the dog immediately jumped into her lap, licking at her face, happy to see her.

Coop was whispering into Amere's ear when a lumberjack-sized fellow approached the car.

"I'll bet you $250,000 that my hog will kill all four of your best dogs."

"Let me see the hog first."

It was the man's land. The hog pen was deeper in the woods, where the dirt road ended and became weeds. My brother parked, and they all got out, including Lucky.

"Put him back in the car."

"Get back in there!"

Lucky did as Jasmine said, then stuck his head out of the window. The hog was out of its pen. It was huge.

"Hell naw! My dogs ain't fighting that!"

"You look like a big spender; a million to your 250?"

The hog started sniffing the air, then charged at Jasmine, smelling Lucky's scent on her. Coop pulled his gun, but the hog was so fast that if Coop had pulled the trigger, it was possible he would've hit Jasmine, who ran around the car.

Lucky broke the window getting out of the car, then attacked the hog, making it stop in its tracks.

Amere was screaming, "Shoot it! Shoot the muthafucka!"

Jasmine was also screaming at Coop,

"Don't shoot Lucky!"

But Coop still didn't have an angle.

A.J. quickly opened the cages of the other dogs that immediately attacked the hog, which excited the owner of the hog.

"We've got us a bet!" Smiling, showing his rotten and missing teeth.

The dogs were biting chunks out of the hog, hurting it. But when the hog's snout hit one of the dogs, its teeth cut the dog to the bone. Blood was everywhere, but the dogs kept attacking. The hog hit one dog across the neck, killing it instantly. Another pit was locked in on the hog's side, eating a hole in it, but the hog reached back and bit it on the back of the neck. The bones could be heard cracking as the dog was killed.

"Two left, gal!"

The hog's focus was on the larger pit in front of it. The pit was locked on the snout of the hog, while half of Lucky's body and his entire head were inside the hole in the hog's side. Somehow, the hog used the strength of its neck to toss the dog into the air, biting it from its chest to its neck, splitting it open. The dog was dead when it hit the ground.

The hog then reached back and tried to bite at Lucky's hind legs, but fell over dead as Lucky backed out of the hole in the side of the hog, pulling out with him what looked like the hog's heart.

Lucky then staggered over to Jasmine and sat, its white coat covered with blood, with more blood pumping out of the deep cuts all over its body.

Amere saw his daughter crying as she picked up her dog, cradling him.

"Give me my muthafuckin' money before I kill you!"

Chapter 46
Commitment Vs Temptation.

I was in my own world at Tiny Tots. It was Easter weekend. The rush had wiped out most of the inventory. I'd just locked the gate behind the last employee and returned to my girls.

"Dad, you've been working really hard. Maybe you and Mom need a romantic vacation?"

"Yeah, and Mommy and I can play in the sand." Ivy didn't understand what Melody was saying.

"No. We're going to stay here. I'll watch her while you guys have fun."

Banging on the gate got our attention. It was Hazel, looking sexier than usual. At first, the girls were excited to see her. Hazel's hand touched each of their shoulders as if she saw them.

"Hey, ladies." Then Hazel's eyes settled on me. They seemed different, hungry, and determined. "Will you join me for a late-night drink, so we can talk?" She took both of my hands in hers. Her touch was soft and sensual.

"I need to finish this. But we can talk here."

Melody was staring at my hands, which Hazel was still holding. Ivy had moved closer to my side but was frowning at Hazel.

Hazel took a deep breath as if ready to dive into uncertainty.

"For you to really heal, you have to have a purpose greater than yourself. That's when you will begin to heal. I want to be that purpose."

"I have a greater purpose. My children, my family."

"You're holding your daughters back from going to the next stage of existence–"

"Dad, don't listen to her. She doesn't know what she's talking about!"

Hazel continued stressing her point.

"Release them, and start over with me. Travel the world with me on my world tour. It's my last tour. Then, if things go as I expect, you can get a divorce and marry me. Start your own law firm in L.A."

The entire time, my girls had been tugging at my wrist, fighting to tear them away from Hazel's hands, screaming at me.

"Daddy, I want to be with you! Daddy, don't leave us!"

"Daddy, we're your motivation! We're your purpose!"

"I love my girls and my wife! I'll never leave my family!" The loudness of my own voice scared me.

Hazel kept her smile and stayed calm.

"That's what I love about you; you love so hard, deep, and forever. Remember, you still have love for me." She kissed me, then left.

Chapter 47
Choice and Consequences.

Jasmine was at home alone, nervously waiting by the door, when her cell rang. It was Jackson Wallace calling at the last minute, "... As much as I want to take you, be there with you I can't. I can't risk the exposure. But I'll pay for everything."

"Are you muthafuckin' serious!"

"Yes, baby. Think about it. Exposure would destroy everything I'm fighting for. I want to be there–"

Jasmine ended the call with him in mid-sentence, then dialed Angel while shedding angry tears.

"I need you to take me."

"That sorry son of a bitch!"

"I know, but can you take me?"

"I can't. Since my mom caught A.J. over, she's been checking my room every hour. I'm sorry."

"It's cool."

"Call me when you get back so I'll know you're okay."

A.J. was at a baseball camp hosted by the batting coach of the Birmingham Barons when he heard his cell phone's ringtone. It was Jasmine's tone, so he had to answer it.

"I'm at practice."

"I know. I need a favor."

"What's what?"

"I need you to take me somewhere right now."

"Are you crying? What's wrong?"

"I'll tell you when you get here."

The coaches saw A.J. packing his belongings.

"James, we're not done."

"It's an emergency. I'll try to make the second half."

As soon as A.J. drove up to the house, Jasmine came out.

"Take me to the clinic."

"What for?"

Tears fell down Jasmine's face.

"I'm having an abortion."

A.J. drove off angrily, gripping the steering wheel.

"For who?"

"Please don't ask me any questions. Not right now. Please?"

Protestors were in front of the abortion clinic, led by Preston.

A.J. and Jasmine pretended to be picketers, then snuck into the clinic.

A.J. didn't judge; he just supported Jasmine's decision. He cried along with her while holding her hand as the doctor used a vacuum-like machine on her.

The entire two hours Jasmine had to rest, A.J. remained by her side.

As A.J. and Jasmine were leaving the clinic, Preston confronted them,

"You don't know what you've done."

"You don't either. Move, man!" A.J. forced their way through the crowd.

Chapter 48
Divided Allegiance.

Amere was attending a meeting with members of some of the most influential groups in Birmingham; they were in the conference room of AME. The minister had the floor.

"Brother Jackson Wallace's agenda and ours go hand in hand. If we stop funding his advertisements now, we risk losing to a person with the exact opposite views. We've worked hard and long and have invested too much to get this opportunity to abandon Jackson Wallace now."

"I for one, don't want Jackson Wallace representing me, my community, and certainly not my business interest–"

The Minister seemed really to go to blows with my brother,

"He has survived the smear campaign. His character is–"

"His character is some shit! Jackson Wallace is scum and should be behind bars or dead. I recommend we cut all ties with Jackson Wallace, and approach Ellis Collins to run for mayor on the best behalf of the city and our interests as businessmen and women."

Derina Boley was there representing the Happy Hour Fund.

"I say we put it to a vote."

The minister was pissed; it could be heard in his tone,

"All right. All in favor of cutting ties with Jackson Wallace, raise your hand." Out of the 21 representatives, nine raised their hands.

"We stay our course."

Amere stood. "Don't consider my businesses as a part of this organization any longer. And I will be withdrawing my funds."

Derina Boley and the other seven members stood in agreement and left along with my brother.

Chapter 49
Crisis and Confrontation.

Angel had snuck out of her bedroom window and gone to comfort Jasmine, who was at home alone.

The emotional pain, plus the feeling that she'd taken an innocent life, had Jasmine severely depressed. Just lying in bed crying to Angel,

"How could he treat me like this? He said he loved me."

Angel knew Jackson Wallace was Jasmine's first heartbreak, "It's going to be all right. It's going to be all right."

Angel couldn't stay long, and as soon as she left, Jasmine went to her parents' medicine cabinet and got some prescription medication.

In bed, Jasmine spelled out Jackson Wallace's name with the pills, then took one pill after the other until she'd taken them all.

Belle and Amere arrived home at the same time, both gritting their teeth at each other as they entered their home.

"If you want a divorce, it's fine with me. You can have whatever you want. I'm sick of all this fighting shit."

My brother was tired. He was trying to do what was right by Belle.

Belle looked at him like he was crazy or on drugs,

"I ain't divorcing your ass. We're gonna work this shit out!"

"So why in the hell are you looking so mad?"

"I'm fixing to kill your daughter. Preston came by the bank and told me she was at the abortion clinic. Jasmine! She's here because her car is out there." Belle and Amere both went to Jasmine's room.

"Don't be acting like you're asleep!" Belle shook Jasmine's shoulder then instantly started screaming once Jasmine's arm fell lifelessly to the side of the bed.

Amere noticed the empty prescription bottle, then scooped up his daughter.

"C'mon!"

Belle rushed to the doors as Amere ran to the car.

The doctors were waiting at the emergency room door when Amere pulled up to the entrance. They rushed Jasmine straight to an examination room, but wouldn't allow Belle or Amere into the room.

Belle was so emotional that Amere had to console her.

"She's going to be all right. She's going to be all right."

A doctor stepped into the lobby.

"We successfully pumped her stomach. She's going to be fine. But we have to keep her over might for a psychiatric evaluation. Do you have an idea of why your daughter would want to kill herself?"

"We think she had an abortion today. Can we see her?"

"Yes, but she's resting."

The doctor escorted them to the room. Jasmine was asleep until she felt Amere stroking her hair. Her eyes opened to see the tears in her father's eyes.

"I'm sorry, Dad. I'm sorry."

"Don't worry about it. It's going to be fine. It's going to be fine."

Belle kissed her daughter's face and then got into bed with her.

"It's going to be fine."

Before the hour had passed, Pearl and I had arrived, then the others: my mother, Viola, and A.J., Angel, and April, then, unexpectedly, Monte arrived, still in his practice gear from the baseball camp. Amere immediately sucka punched Monte, then started beating him, until A.J. and I were able to pull him off. Jasmine's crying and screaming were deafening.

"It wasn't him! It was Jackson Wallace!"

Pearl immediately started crying while she hugged Jasmine.

No one tried to stop Amere from leaving; instead, all the men in the room went with him.

Coop and several street fighters met us at Jackson Wallace's campaign headquarters. Jackson Wallace was in a meeting with two businessmen and his wife when Amere entered the office, then immediately commenced to beating Jackson Wallace's ass all over the room. Hard, tooth-rattling punches, felt and rights hooks. Haymakers. Amere was like a man possessed with no regard for the people in the room.

Jackson Wallace tried to fight back, but he was too much of a diplomat, plus, Amere's hands were too much for him.

Jackson Wallace stumbled out of the office into the main section, where the volunteer phone line operators were, who started screaming because Amere wouldn't stop beating Jackson Wallace, who was trying his best to put distance between himself and my brother. He was looking for help when he noticed Coop and the street fighters had his bodyguards sitting in chairs, daring them to move.

Jackson Wallace tried to run for the door, but I tripped him. Amere sat in Jackson Wallace's chest and beat him unconscious. He would've beaten him to death if Coop hadn't pulled Amere off of Jackson Wallace.

"Muthafucka, you come near my daughter or anybody in my family again, I'll kill you!"

Amere was arrested but was released before I could get to the station.

Jackson Wallace had become conscious and refused to press charges. He knew Amere wouldn't dare expose Jasmine to the negative publicity of having an abortion.

Chapter 50
I'll Show You How to Play Dirty.

Jackson Wallace was banged up pretty bad, lying in his bed, when he noticed his wife was packing her suitcase. He was too sore to attempt to stop her.

She looked at him like he was disgusting.

"You would rather be with a child than me!"

"You don't understand."

"I don't. I don't understand how you could be so sick! Amere should've killed you."

"Gone go! You'll be back."

She looked at him as if she wanted to kill him, then left but she knew he was telling the truth.

It was mid-summer before Jackson Wallace was well enough to make a public appearance. Being out of sight had actually helped his campaign. His name and ideas had buzzed even louder in his absence. And the huge crowd at his rally welcomed his return.

"… What are the barriers that need to be removed? We have to ask what it will take to accelerate progress. …" He glanced over the crowd of faces, then noticed Jasmine's, smiling at him.

"The flame we have started must not be allowed to burn out!"

Jackson Wallace finished his speech, then shook hands and kissed the babies and ladies while making his way to Jasmine. But she was gone.

When Jackson Wallace got the limo, the driver gave him a note from Jasmine.

"I'm so sorry about what my dad did to you. I want to see you, be with you so badly it hurts. But nowhere in the city. Your hideaway. I'll meet you there in an hour." All Jackson Wallace could think about was sweet revenge on Amere.

When he showed up at the cabin, Jasmine's car was there. He roughly sexed Jasmine, trying to hurt her while calling her daddy's little girl the entire time but he exhausted himself and fell asleep afterwards, which gave Jasmine the opportunity to get the surveillance footage from the hotel of Jackson Wallace forcing Pearl into the hotel room.

As if everything was fine, Jasmine woke up Jackson Wallace with a kiss.

"I'm leaving before my parents get worried."

Jasmine went directly to the post office and mailed the dics.

Chapter 51
Real Love.

Belle had talked Amere into fighting, instead of just allowing nature to take its course. She went to every chemotherapy session with him, cleaned up the vomit, and held his hand.

My brother had started losing weight and his hair. Belle bought him a new wardrobe and cut his hair down to a shadow to match his beard. She kept him flying and his spirit up. She even allowed Viola to come over, but stayed by his side the entire visit.

On my brother's sickest nights, Belle would cradle him and rock him to sleep.

"I love you, Belle."

"I know. I know."

Chapter 52
Embracing the Unseen.

Even with Hazel gone on her world tour, my marriage was still rocky, but we were trying to stabilize it.

Melody would watch Ivy while Pearl and I would have our date nights.

The small affection of talking over dinner, touching her hand, led to Pearl attending therapy with me.

My girls normally hated going to therapy, but it was a tell-all session.

"They're not in my imagination. I'm not having conversations with myself. I see them, hear them. I can feel them–"

"That is your mind denying the fact that they are dead."

"Dad, let's go. I don't like her."

"Daddy, why can't mommy see us? Does mommy still love us?" It was all messy: Annette, my daughters, what was reality?

"Yes, she does. They're real. They exist!"

"No and yes. They exist because your mind creates–"

I cut off Annette in mid-sentence.

"Be quiet! Close your eyes, Pearl. Close your eyes, please?"

Melody began running her fingers through her mother's hair. Pearl somewhat shivered, then relaxed.

"Do you feel that?"

"Yes. It's cold but gentle."

"That's Mclody playing with your hair."

Annette saw the tears released from Pearl's eyes and watched, amazed, as the tears on Pearl's cheeks disappeared. Ivy was wiping them away as she sat in her mother's lap.

"Don't cry, Mommy."

Pearl felt Ivy and sensed who it was, "My baby, my baby!" More tears poured down Pearl's face as she embraced Ivy, then Melody, "I've missed y'all so much." Annette only stared, not fully understanding how or what was taking place.

Chapter 53
Special Delivery.

Ellis Collins returned to his desk to find the box addressed to him with no return address.

"Who put this here?"

"I did. It came in the mail."

Ellis Collins suspiciously opened it to find the disc.

Other detectives were interested in what was in the box.

"What've you got there?"

"I'm not sure."

"Let's find out."

"No. I'm late for a meeting."

Ellis Collins didn't have a meeting; he was still pissed that the ecstasy lab had burned down and Pho had gone missing a day before the raid. Supposedly, only a handful had known of the operation. He wasn't about to risk another leak, even if he didn't know what was on the disc.

Ellis Collins went home to view it. His mother-in-law came into the den and stopped once she recognized it was of Pearl and Jackson Wallace. The footage was of Jackson Wallace somewhat forcing Pearl out of the car, almost dragging her into the hotel to the elevator, then to the hotel room.

"I knew that child was telling the truth!" His mother-in-law's sentiment was the same as his own.

Ellis Collins still didn't go straight to the captain. He wanted to make sure the case was concrete before he mentioned the evidence to anyone. He tracked down and questioned the former clerk of the hotel,

"Sir, I have some questions for you pertaining to–"

"I'm running late for work. Can we do this another time?"

"I'll tell you how I can do it: I can charge you with being an accessory to rape, and you can answer the questions in front of a jury. Or you can tell me the truth right now, and I'll see that you get immunity."

With all the pieces, Pearl's testimony, the clerk's testimony, and the surveillance footage, Ellis Collins presented it to the police captain, who reluctantly gave the nod to take the evidence to a grand jury.

Chapter 54
I Would've Been Great at It.

I don't know how Jackson Wallace knew, but he'd sent everyone home.

His campaign headquarters was deserted. He, himself, was in his office at his desk on the phone with the judge.

"... I've always tried to make you proud. I'm sorry about being such a disgrace... Yes, I am ..." Pinching his nose, Jackson Wallace fought back tears.

"... But my vision was what would've been best for Birmingham. I'm not perfect. One or two flaws are nothing compared to the good I would have accomplished as mayor. Hold on, Dad. ..."

Jackson Wallace heard the door handle being turned, then he picked up the 9-millimeter that was lying on his desk, which he quickly pointed at Ellis Collins, who entered with the indictment in his hand.

"... Dad, I love you. I've got to go. I have business to handle. Bye." Ellis Collins was still staring at Jackson Wallace and the gun. The expression on Jackson Wallace's face was so calm, it was demented.

"Jackson Wallace, you're under arrest for rape."

The news didn't seem to bother Jackson Wallace. He even smirked.

"The difference between us is that I live life like I want. I make the rules. And I'm going to die like I want. You will never be more than me. I'll be remembered long after you've been forgotten. And when they do remember you, it'll be the ambitious policemen who tried to smear me. You'll never be mayor. You've smeared yourself. Your hands are dirty in everyone's eyes."

Then Jackson Wallace put the gun in his own mouth and blew out his own brains.

Chapter 55
Until Death Do Us Apart.

Justice had been served, and Pearl and I had decided to renew our vows. My brother was to be my best man again, and Belle was to be one of Pearl's bridesmaids. It was to be held on Amere's ranch.

The day of the ceremony, Amere was in the bathroom of his home getting dressed while talking on his cell phone,

"... Mom, yes, the chemo has me a little tired, but I'm fine. ..."

Belle entered the bedroom with Amere's shirt and then opened the bathroom door to hear better.

"Who are you talking to?"

"Yeah, that's her."

"See, I've let this bitch come see you a few times, now she's taking my kindness for weakness."

"She's trippin' over nothing. ... I know. I love you, too."

"Goddamnit! You're going to tell her you love her like I ain't even here?"

"That's not necessary. ... Fine. Here, crazy ass woman."

Amere extended the cell phone toward Belle's face.

"She wants to talk to you."

"I don't want to talk to her crazy ass. I ain't about to let y'all ruin my day. Here!"

Belle shoved the shirt into Amere's chest, which caught him off guard and he stumbled backwards and lost his balance, then fell and hit his head on the edge of the tub. Amere was instantly dead, and Belle knew. She just started screaming and crying, screaming and crying.

Jasmine came into the room half-dressed, then ran to her father, "Mama, go call the ambulance! Go call the ambulance!"

My mother had been on the phone with Amere, had heard the entire conversation, and knew his death was an accident, but her knowledge didn't stop the pain of losing my brother for none of us.

Amere's funeral had a huge turnout. Many tears were shed, and many kind words were said over my brother. Everyone had a high regard for him. I stayed long after the dirt had been packed on my brother's casket. Something was telling me to wait. The rest of my family was in the limos, waiting but giving time to say my goodbyes.

Chapter 56
My Moment Alone with My Big Brother.

Each of my daughters had one of my hands. The sun was starting to set, casting shadows, which seemed like Amere stepped out of one. He had a shine about him, smiling as he strolled my way as if nothing had ever been wrong with him.

"Don't be sad, man. And don't blame her. I was dying anyway. Chemo was killing me ...."

Amere became amazed -- he was finally able to see my daughters.

"I seriously thought you were crazy talking about how you could see the girls." He hugged them both.

"Remember, you promised to take care of mine. I promise to take care of yours."

I couldn't control my tears. My girls had started to glow.

"Don't cry, bro. We're always going to be with you."

Amere hugged me, and a tingle went through my body, a peacefulness.

"I know."

Melody's tears looked like diamonds; we all knew it was a parting.

"Dad, it's time for us to go. Mom will take care of you. I'll always love you, Dad."

I picked up Ivy, and she kissed away my tears, then blew a gooseberry on my cheek until I started laughing. She then stared at my face and nodded like a grown-up.

"I like it when you laugh, Daddy. Uncle Amere is going to show us a good time."

Then Ivy blew another gooseberry on my cheek to keep me from crying.

Amere took my baby.

"Maybe you can talk crazy ass Belle into seeing Annette."

"I doubt it."

"Me too. I love you. Now go take care of our families. We're good here. I've got this. C'mon, girls, let's go see how much hell we can raise in Heaven."

I turned to walk toward the limos, then stopped and turned around in time to see them fade into the sunset.

Never the end, only a new beginning.

Smeared by Johnnie E Sanders

HUMAN NATURE

Chapter 1
The Devil Himself Is a Fallen Angel

Urban Warfare.

Certain aspects of life you have to remind yourself it isn't right, it shouldn't be happening; or you become numb from seeing such dramatic events so regularly that they seem normal.

The rainy season had set in. Birmingham was drenched, but we carried on like normal, seeing but not seeing. Not caring would describe it better. Two police cars and a Humvee; the jump-out task force team was cruising the streets of a residential area. All the houses were old but huge. The sun hadn't quite set. On the porch of a particular home was an elderly man; to his side, behind the large potted plant, was an AK-47.

A youngster was playing with a pit bull on the sidewalk near a rusty, old, broken-down car. Under his shirt in the waist of his jeans was a 9-millimeter, and under the car was another AK-47. They were both actually on post, guarding the outside perimeter of the home.

A sniper bullet struck the old man by the door in the center of his forehead, splattering blood on the siding of the house.

Another bullet ripped through the throat of the youngster, making the dog nervously jump back.

The jump-out unit scooped onto the property and stormed the house.

Their armored suits covered their bodies and concealed their faces. Inside the house, there were people counting money and packaging drugs oblivious until the unit had moved in, sweeping from floor to floor, room to room, killing everything and everybody in their path. Some tried to surrender, thinking they would be arrested instead of killed, but they were wrong; the bullets sprayed them anyway. The team was tactical, merciless, and highly efficient. Some secured the house while others bagged the money, but didn't touch the dope. In a matter of seconds, the entire operation was over, and the unit had departed the scene as quickly as they had arrived.

Country was a 32-year-old sergeant in the Army Reserve, a sniper with the body of an overweight cook, gentle and harmless looking. He wasn't dumb or brilliant but somewhere in between; smart enough to self-medicate with liquor, bottle after bottle, to black out his confusion from killing nightmares, sleeplessness, and anxiety. He and his unit had toured twice in Iraq and twice in Afghanistan within a 60-month period. He suffered from emotional trauma, PTSD, brought on by what he'd seen and done in the wars.

Country's wife, Lulu, would awaken in the middle of the night to Country's loud weeping to finally find him in the corner of the kitchen, naked, balled up like a scared little child.

Country hadn't been ordered to treatment, but it was a way for him to guarantee he was fit if his unit was deployed again. The Army was his safe haven. In life, he was a nobody, not even average. But in combat, he excelled. He was good at killing. He knew if he had a middle-of-the-night episode while on tour, he would officially be labeled with PTSD and his career in the service would be limited, if not over. Plus, the fact that he worked as a janitor at the Birmingham Police Department, which meant the city covered the cost of therapy -- Country used it to his advantage and met weekly with Dr. Annette Wright. On her couch, he could release his rage and justify why.

"War releases the animal in you. Instincts take over, and we fight for survival. It's like you don't care about anything or anyone except yourself, and who or what's yours. You feel nothing. Couldn't care less what happens to anyone or anything else. You do what you have to do. If you allow shame or remorse or even the thought to slip into your head, you're dead! Your unit is dead! That's how we survive! Then they bring us home and want us to act civilized. Like it never happened."

"Like what never happened?"

Country couldn't articulate what his mind wouldn't admit he'd done.

"To carry out orders!"

Annette could physically see Country's frustration mounting as he tried to restrain his rage, gripping the edge of the couch with both hands.

"... Defend our country! Complete the mission!"

"Breathe. Breathe. You are in control. You are in control."

He took deep breaths, calming himself.

"Yes, I am ... Thanks, Doc. Same time next week?"

Chapter 2
The Rhythm of Struggling.

The University of Alabama at Birmingham had made itself interdependent with the city. Its campus stretched from Compass Bank to Greensprings. Four white male students were strolling in the parking lot of the music hall as if it wasn't pouring rain. To take a closer look at them, they had the appearance of misfits, slackers actually, they were musicians, members of the symphony and had been since elementary school.

Their sizes would've made you think they were more into sports, but music was their love. Classical music was their way to get a free education, but hip-hop was their dream of riches and fame. They were a rap group slash band; each could sing, rap, and play all the instruments. They'd actually independently produced a CD, but because they were too educated and conscious, the labels had rejected their demos. The leader of their group was Scott, a 20-year-old who had a mixture of trailer park trash attitude with a confident swagger of determination. He was the premier rapper and self-proclaimed manager of the group. Contrary to their appearance, the CD was fire.

The group had started getting popular on social media, which had helped to get their CD placed in the mom and pop music stores around the city but mostly they moved the CDs themselves—sold them outside the hot spots in the city with the help of Scott's wife, Candy, who looked out of his league being super dark and super fine. Candy always pitched the hardest.

"More like the reincarnation of Young Ryder or Tupac. Buy it. If you don't like it, you can get your money back. ... I'll see you at home."

......

The rain had taken a temporary break. Night had consumed the city. The city's outskirts, a rural area, was almost completely pitched black, even the campus of one of the mega churches except for the flashlights of the four masked figures loading valuables out of the church into a white van.

Once the van was completely packed with candle holders, crosses, gold trays, stands, and picture frames, the figures went back inside and splashed the place with diesel fuel and set it afire.

As the white van entered onto the freeway, the four figures removed their masks, revealing Scott and the three other group members. Scott drove to a paint shop located in downtown Birmingham, where all four of them worked. It was three o'clock in the morning, and no one else was there. The owner trusted them and relied on them so much that he'd given them a set of keys. Two members packed the items from the van into bags and loaded them onto the back of Big CJ's pick-up.

Scott quietly entered his home, a one-bedroom apartment in the central city's projects. He tried to ease into bed, but his toddler daughter woke up, hugging Scott's neck, which woke up Candy.

They all shared the medium-sized bed that took up most of the small, cramped room.

"I'm working a double tomorrow. Pick up Sadie from Ms. Brown after you get off."

Candy was a waitress slash singer. She believed in herself and Scott, and did whatever she could to help with the studio cost and the bills around their apartment and in their life.

Chapter 3
A Moral Dilemma.

I'm Devin James, attorney at law. I'd been on a hiatus from practicing law to resolve some emotional issues I'd had. But I was back, not as a public defender, I'd accepted a partnership with an elder frat brother of mine who had mentored me while I attended law school.

Of course, the idea of having a corner office with a view of the entire city had me enthused, along with the seven figures I was receiving, but at the same time, I was leery about defending someone who could afford the retainer fee of the firm.

It was my first day as part of the firm, and I was summoned to a meeting with Emory Collins, the founder of the firm, who was also the uncle of Detective Ellis Collins. His office made mine look like a coat closet.

"...This is a high, high-profile case, but I'm sure it'll be nothing to you." Emory's smile, age, and encouraging demeanor could've been read as manipulative or motivational. He had the perfect poker face and knew it. So I scanned through the file. It was my old elementary school basketball coach.

He'd been charged with sexual assault of a female elementary school basketball player. Coach was also a Hall-of-fame pro basketball player who had won championships with the 76ers and the Lakers.

Since I was reading and hadn't spoken, Emory started to stroke my ego, "He personally asked for you to represent him."

It was hard not to look at the case through the eyes of a father, plus I'd promised myself I wouldn't knowingly get a monster off so I met with Coach at his lake house in the woods to see what my intuition had to say.

Coach was fishing from the bank of the lake with a fire blazing and a line of fish waiting to be cooked. He had a kind of inexplicable charisma, an energy about himself that other people just don't have. He seemed to be in high spirits, but his body language said otherwise.

"... Maybe I should've settled when her gold digger of a mutha..." He stopped from cursing. "... propositioned me."

"Why?"

"Then I would still have the joy of my life: coaching kids, helping develop them. ..."

He hadn't actually coached in decades, he micromanaged, almost like an AD of the private elementary school he was part owner of which was a basketball factory for a bigger basketball factory high school that guaranteed all their players, both boys and girls, would go to Division 1 universities or better, the pros.

"... I didn't touch that child. I swear on Betty's soul. It's hard enough for me to piss, let alone think about anything else. ..." He realized I hadn't made up my mind whether I was representing him or not. "... I've been helping the program by networking with the high school. ..." What he meant was that he relocated the families and the talented young athletes. "... She and her evil ass mother are in one of my properties right now. And she had the nerve to ask for my house and $5 million! I can't even put them out!"

Nothing sounded unbelievable, so I took it as it was possible he hadn't done it.

Chapter 4
Passion and Intrigue.

Detective Ellis Collins and Dr. Annette Wright had been dating for years. Everything they did showed how deeply they loved each other. Annette was ready for the next stage of their relationship; Ellis Collins was too, but something kept him from popping the question. He was my best friend and frat brother and had told me he was ready. All of his excuses for waiting had run out. Ebony, his daughter, was now a freshman in college. Annette and his mother-in-law from his first marriage, who lived with Ellis Collins, got along great, but something wouldn't allow him. It was the fear of another person seeking revenge, and Ellis Collins had to relive the horror and the guilt of losing his wife. It had been over a decade, but his wife's death still haunted him.

The night had been perfect for Annette and Ellis Collins. Dinner, dancing, even the rain made it seem romantic; dashing for Ellis Collins' car, being soaked by the time he and Annette reached the front door of Annette's home.

Their passion was feverish, undressing from the time they entered the house, being completely naked by the time they reached her bedroom.

With all the professionalism and control Annette personified as a doctor in the office, disappeared in the bedroom; she was a woman who wanted a man who took control, somewhat manhandled her, exactly the way Ellis Collins put it down. At times, their lovemaking seemed animalistic, but they both loved it and each other, knowing when to be rough and when to be sensual.

Starting another round of caveman meets cavewoman, Annette and Ellis Collins knocked the lamp off the nightstand next to the bed. The bedroom door opened, and a red dot in the dark shone on Ellis Collins' chest. He saw the figure in the doorway and moved toward his holster to be tazed. The electric shock knocked him off his feet. The figure quickly turned on the light.

"C'mon! ..." A grey-haired old pretty woman in a house robe. She then realized Annette was naked, wrapped in a sheet, standing over Ellis Collins, who was gaining his composure. "... I thought someone was in here killing you. All the noise you two were making." She tried to be subtle, peeping at Ellis Collins's erection.

"What are you doing here, Grandma? You texted that you'd cancelled your trip."

"You know I'm old school. I meant the flight was cancelled, but I was able to catch an earlier one. Since you gave me a key and you weren't here, I let myself in. You two keep it down. We'll talk in the morning. I'm sorry about that, baby." She was somewhat smiling at Ellis Collins, who was catching his breath on the edge of the bed.

Annette's day was going great. She'd arrived at her office to be greeted by a bouquet of roses with a card from Ellis Collins inviting her to lunch. None of her patients had had setbacks. And to her surprise, Ellis Collins arrived wearing a new suit. "We have to leave now. Our reservation at Azure is at 12."

The restaurant Azure wasn't Ellis Collins' normal taste or budget. It was a five-star restaurant with super exposure. She knew he was going to propose, but when they stepped into the parking structure on the level of her office, she saw her 70-plus-year-old grandmother driving an up-to-date model rental car, pulling onto their level of the parking structure.

"Grandma, what are you doing driving?"

"I don't like smelling old people, so the bus was out. Plus, I wanted to do some shopping. I need a new wig and hat. I thought maybe you wanted to join me for shopping and lunch."

Before Annette could answer, Ellis Collins kissed her cheek, "Babe, go ahead. We wouldn't make our reservation now anyway."

Annette's grandmother noticed the obvious disappointment in Annette, "I don't want to intrude if you two already had plans."

Ellis Collins kissed grandma's cheek. "Don't worry yourself. We have all the time in the world. You two enjoy yourselves."

"What do you mean by that?"

Ellis Collins knew he'd worded it wrong, and it showed on his face, "I mean, I just want you to enjoy your time with your granddaughter."

"What does that mean?"

Ellis Collins kept his mouth shut and just kissed the old lady's cheek again.

"Don't make it seem as if I'm about to die, because I'm not."

Chapter 5
Silent Ruthlessness.

Country returned to work. His cold-bloodedness was so concealed that no one even guessed he could be so ruthless. He was the supervisor over the janitors at the police department, so he went unhampered and was conveniently invisible around the precinct. Instead of wearing slacks and ties, he preferred wearing the janitor's overalls and did the major cleaning assignments himself because he didn't trust anyone to do the job well enough. The main hallway floors looked like glass, but Country continued buffing them until his assistant, Bo, who did wear a shirt and a tie, pulled the cord out of the wall electrical unit.

"Lulu called and left this for you." Bo passed the note, then waited, reading Country's pitiful expression as Country read the note. "Man, it ain't that bad. Go home and put a suit on. This place will survive without you. I've got this."

Country had forgotten the e-commerce seminar he and his wife had registered for and paid for. A waste of time and money was his opinion of it. He was quite satisfied with himself and his financial life. But he didn't believe in wasting anything, especially his time and money.

By the time Country arrived at the hotel ballroom where the seminar was being held, people were actually leaving. Country's posture and the suit he had on made him appear very distinguished. He spotted his wife laughing and talking to a nerdy-looking white man, whom Country recognized as the person giving the seminar, and a fly brother in his forties. Country loved his wife like a man loves his muscle car; more like a prized possession, and was super protective of anyone getting too close. Most people, once they got to know them as a couple, couldn't understand how she had fallen for him. Lulu and Country had met in elementary school. They were the only two white students at Norwood. Both were somewhat from dirt-broke, dysfunctional families—they were drawn to one another.

The skirt suit Lulu had on was conservative but form-fitting, revealing how extremely sexy she was.

Country felt out of his element around businessmen and enterprising individuals and even more berated and inadequate once he was close enough to hear their conversation.

"... It's definitely the guide to making money."

It all sounded like bragging to Country, which was putting him into a violent mood caused by frustration that he only understood. But Lulu had learned his anti-social behaviors the hard way, and recognized the signs of his spectrum of emotions; his clenched fists she knew he was about to lose it, especially once Phil unconsciously touched her shoulder while agreeing.

Lulu quickly embraced Country, "Let me introduce you to my husband, Madison. This is Joel Comm, and this is Phil Robertson of Robertson's hardware stores. He's actually our neighbor."

"Your wife is an extraordinary marketeer. We would love for you two to join us for dinner."

"Nooo!" Lulu knew Country wouldn't be able to keep it together for an entire meal. "I've taken up enough of both of your time with my questions. I'm going to at least let you two enjoy your meal."

Country's scowl quickly disappeared as the men looked to him. "Seems like they can't get enough of your questions."

"It's my treat."

Country focused on Phil, then gave a half-hearted smile. "How can we refuse?"

"Good. We can all ride in the limo."

"No. We'll follow you."

Country kept his smile the entire time he and his wife were in the presence of Joel and Phil, but once he and Lulu entered their vehicle, Country slapped blood out of Lulu's mouth.

"Don't ever let another man touch you in any form or fashion!" Then, in a matter of microseconds, Country's anger had shifted, as if he was puzzled how Lulu didn't understand why. "You know they're just trying to play you for a fool. They don't care about your honor. I do."

"Let's just go home. Please?"

Chapter 6
Courage.

Annette somewhat looked forward to her sessions with Country. She found him morally admirable but also depressed or troubled. But she wasn't certain if he had a mental illness disorder, because he had a conscience that seemingly kept him in line.

Often, Annette didn't have to ask questions; she just redirected Country's questions for him to answer himself.

"There are times when having integrity begins to feel like you're playing the fool," Country was venting, while pacing in a short three-step, then turning around style.

"How do you mean?"

"How can any of us live as we all do, among so many destructive liars, con artists, parasites, and not confront them, do something, or even notice it!" Country's convictions were what captivated her.

"How would you have it?"

"I think we should handle it as we do in war."

"But is this a time of war?"

"Yes! It's a war between good and evil."

"But people are killed in wars. Is that how you would handle so many destructive liars, con artists, and parasites?"

"Someone in authority gives the order."

Annette understood that most soldiers believed that if the commands came from a legitimate authority, the soldiers weren't responsible, but only carried out orders, a divine loophole that most people use when asked to do something bad in order to bring about something else that is deemed good.

So again, Country was showing signs of a rational consciousness, not mental illness.

But she also knew conscience, combined with surpassing moral courage, could create a demon or an angel.

The bell rang, ending the session.

"Same time next week, Doc?"

"Yes, Sergeant Madison."

Twice a week, after work, Annette and my wife, Pearl, held a free workshop for abused women at the recreation center in the Gate City projects. The workshop was really open to any woman who had the strength to come.

"The most destructive part of him is his personality. If his charm and sexuality and his role-playing somehow fail, he uses fear and physical abuse to get his way. ..."

Annette paused, glancing over the painful anguish that showed on the faces of the women in the audience, whose tears and nods expressed how deeply right she was.

"... Then after he has put his hands on you, he doesn't apologize but somehow redirects the blame at you for making him have such an outburst. ..." Lulu was in the back of the gym, wearing big shades covering her swollen, blackened eye. Instead of sitting, she leaned on the wall next to the exit, as if she was about to leave at any second.

"... But as long as he feels respected or at least feared, which masquerades brilliantly as respect, he is the loving husband or boyfriend. ... In our hearts, we know there is no such thing as a person who is 100 percent good, and so there must be no such thing as a person who is 100 percent bad, so you find yourself forgiving him. Then something triggers the cycle again. ... I'm not advising anyone that your relationship is over. What I am advising is that if you are in an abusive relationship, it is best for you to put distance between

you and your partner until you both can get therapy, and if he refuses, you
should end the relationship."

Chapter 7
Hip-Hop.

Most would've said Scott was a confused youngster, going through a culture crisis, living in the projects, trying to make it as a rapper in a black dominated industry and they all would've been largely wrong; for he had clarity and was totally conscious of what was happening around him and the rest of the world. Scott had no problem expressing his views when asked, even though he was seldom asked, and when he was, it wasn't by anyone his own age. It was mostly people who were his mom or grandma's age that frowned on him, his appearance, his attitude not the hip-hop generation.

Scott's mother and grandmother shared a double-wide trailer in Tarrant City, an annexed part of Birmingham. Their love for Sadie had broken a lot of their biases, but Scott was still aware of the stern stares from their neighbors who lived on the trailer park lot. Not that Scott cared or was even intimidated the least.

Scott's group was at the recording studio, setting up their instruments when he arrived. The sluggish way they were moving, somewhat ignoring him, he sensed the tension and knew the cause.

"I know it seems like I'm putting our career on hold, but I'm not. I'm sticking with the plan to bring out Candy first; it's the same as promoting us. ..."

The others gritted their teeth but were intensely listening.

"... Paying YG to spit on her first track will get mainstream attention. Plus, we're her band. She'll be accepted more easily. We're spitting on three of her other tracks anyway. Man, y'all trippin'. We'll get the exposure being her opening act."

Even though the other members might not have liked the idea, Scott had sound reasoning.

YG was one of the hottest rappers in the game plus they had learned to depend on Scott's judgment.

"How much to get him?"

"Maybe two more licks."

Chapter 8
The Burning Case.

Birmingham had the highest murder rate in the nation, but the church burnings were getting national attention, which brought out all the fame seekers looking for their 15 minutes to shine. It was an embarrassment to the entire state, and phones were ringing and pressure was being applied down the chain of command.

Ellis Collins was already assigned to a major case, which he was having headaches over so when he was called into the captain's office, he was already short-tempered until he saw the mayor and the chief of police.

All were newly elected or appointed. The mayor and Ellis Collins had history.

As a city council representative, she'd opposed several of his crime-solving tactics and, on several occasions, tried to have him fired. But without him, she wouldn't have been elected mayor. It was his investigative skills that had driven her opponent to suicide. She'd rewarded the captain by helping him become the chief of police. The captain's position was offered to Ellis Collins, but he had turned it down because of the politics behind the office, which made the position available for Paris, who was having a hard time adjusting from an A-one crime solver to an ass-kissing flunky. She and Ellis Collins had partnered up on many cases over the years and had become honest and open friends. Ellis Collins could read the stress on Paris' face that she didn't like what she had to say as much as he wouldn't enjoy hearing it.

"Detective Collins, you have been assigned to the church burning case."

"Paris! Captain, I'm up to my ass in bodies from the fake jump-out unit. I don't have time for this."

It really wasn't the case that bothered Ellis Collins; he just didn't want the circus show that came along with it.

The mayor pushed her weight, "Detective Collins, this case is unsettling a region and igniting terror. We need a face and a person the people trust to solve this problem." Ellis Collins understood the mayor's motives; the case was her chance to disgrace him and fire him if he failed. "Fake policemen robbing and killing citizens of Birmingham aren't terrifying?"

"They're drug dealers and criminals that are being killed!"

"It's still murder! There are no bodies in the case you're trying to assign to me."

"That you are assigned to! Unless you're refusing to accept, which is in any case a refusal to do your duty and is grounds for termination." She raised the case file toward Ellis Collins. "… There's a press conference scheduled for 11:30 this morning." Ellis Collins accepted the file while mean-mugging, staring at her.

The Southern Baptist Bible Belt representatives from all the southern states had pitched tents in downtown Birmingham. Several preachers and their congregations, along with local and national news crews, were at the press conference outside of city hall. Ellis Collins was on a first-name basis with all but a few of the reporters, so as soon as he stepped to the podium, the questions started.

"Ellis, are these crimes connected? … Ellis, is there a group of interest? … Ellis, do you have a motive behind these crimes?"

"No comment. … No comment. … No comment."

A particular female journalist, Connie Cox, had forced her way to the front of the crowd.

"Detective Collins, is there anything you can comment on?" Ellis Collins recognized her face. He'd seen her picture next to her editorials in the USA Today newspaper. He'd thought all her articles were overly exaggerated.

"I'm committed to solving this case. But as of now, this case is an ongoing investigation, and it wouldn't be wise for me to tip my hand to the suspects. Thank you all for coming."

Ellis Collins walked away from the podium but stopped once a loudmouth preacher, Preston, seized the opportunity to get national recognition.

"This is a travesty when in this day and age, something as sacrilegious as burning churches is done! We cannot tolerate the hate represented in these crimes."

Smothering smoke still rose from the ruins of the latest church that had been set ablaze.

The firemen had done all they could, but nothing inside the church could be saved. Dawn was breaking. The forensic team had yellow-taped the majority of the area, looking for evidence of the perpetrators, which the cold and the rain-soaked grounds did their best to conceal. Ellis Collins was on the scene, bundled tight in his scarf and coat. He and a member of the forensic team were examining what tire tracks they could find.

"Why do these seem to get deeper? Do your best to make some plates of these."

Chapter 9
A Community's Divide.

I was getting mixed signals on the sexual assault case of the coach from the people I questioned in the community and at the elementary school of the alleged victim.

Everyone thought highly of the young girl and gave only positive feedback about her. Then, without me asking, the negative details came unsolicited about the girl's mother. "What a sweet Angel. The best-behaved child I've ever taught. But you wouldn't think it was possible if you ever had a conversation with her mother."

Even the interviews with the girl's teammates had the same theme: they loved the girl but called her mother the Tiger Mom. I understood growing up with an overly supportive and disciplinarian mother. It wasn't as bad as people made it out to be, plus the child was a superstar, and I knew superstars couldn't do anything wrong in the eyes of their fans.

I'd talked Pearl into attending an elementary school basketball game with me. It had been a while since we'd seen one. Our daughter Melody had attended the same elementary school and played basketball. It brought back fun but sad memories.

The alleged victim was a natural star on the court: great low-post moves, ball-handling skills, and an outside shot, along with a million-dollar smile. She had the entire gym mesmerized until the mother, no older than 26 years of age, entered in glorified hoochie-mama style with four sidekicks just as hoochie-mama.

I wasn't certain if the charges against the coach were even known to the student body or the parents until the crowd grew rowdy toward the mother.

"Ain't any stripper poles in here."

“Naw, she needs to be on Third!”

Third Avenue was a whore stroll. The crowd wasn’t blaming the child or Coach; it was somehow the mother’s fault.

But the mother wasn’t bashful, “I know this punk ass nigga and this nothin’ ass hoe ain’t trying to get ignorant up in here!”

Someone in the crowd used the numbers of the people to shout what they were afraid to say by themselves,

“You are damn wrong for using that child like that.”

“Fuck whoever said it! Y’all the muthafuckas pimpin’ y’all children! Letting that perverted old muthafucka touch on y’all child! My baby’s here to play basketball because she loves it! I don’t need shit they give me!”

“Sit your ass down!”

“Fuck you! Make me sit down with your tough ass!”

A few parents stood, then the mother’s girlfriends did also, showing their support.

“What? I dare y’all to get ignorant up in here!”

The ball game had stopped because the young girl had walked off the court with the ball in her hands. Standing next to her mother, the daughter looked more like a baby sister. They shared the same grimace as well as skin tone and face, and you could see one day soon the hourglass shape.

The young girl was ready to go to war alongside her mother, then school security and the principal hurried over, “Ms. Westly, this isn’t acceptable behavior. I’m going to have to ask you to leave.”

“Muthafucka, I ain’t start this shit! Oh, I see how it is. Fuck your bitch ass, too!” She and her friends started to leave, but she stopped once she noticed her daughter running to the bench for her belongings.

"Naw, baby. You stay and play your game. We ain't gonna let no fuckin' body stop you from doing what you love. Play and have fun. Fuck these people!"

The girl put her backpack down and went back out on the court, and the crowd cheered.

The mother frowned at them, then she and her friends left the gym. The mother was real. I'd felt her sincerity. It had reminded me of my mother on many occasions.

Chapter 10
Chasing Dreams.

Candy and her backup singers felt like they were on top of the world, and they had a good reason to feel that way. The start of their dreams was coming true.

They were recording Candy's first CD.

The backup singers were actually a group that Scott discovered at a local high school talent contest that he'd won. He'd promised to help them cut a CD as soon as Candy's CD caught fire. For now, they were just thrilled to be getting paid to sing on Candy's CD.

Scott and his group were playing their instruments live. Everyone was feeling the vibe, getting into the tracks. Candy had a 1920s retro feel, scatting, sounding classical, then mixing it with a soulful hip-hop blend. So unique and they all flowed so smoothly together that they would lose track of the time, until the sound engineer held up a screaming Sadie, realizing they'd been in the recording booth from midnight until 5:30 in the morning.

For a week straight, they worked tirelessly until the majority of the tracks of Candy's CD were to Scott's liking, and the money for more studio time had run out.

The wear and tear took its toll on Scott, who would fall asleep during lectures in his classes and was impatient during symphony rehearsal. Many a morning, Scott wanted to sleep in, but Candy pushed him and wouldn't allow him.

"Get up! Two more semesters and you graduate. Get up!"

Scott's major was pre-law, something he and Candy were proud of and a safety net for them if their dream fell short. But Scott's love for Candy and music itself made him determined to be successful at music, and so was his group.

With the spotlight on the burning of the churches, Scott and his crew had to be extra cautious, and they knew this especially since Ellis Collins had been assigned to the case. He, Candy, and Sadie would attend the Sunday service of the next targeted Church. Candy was religious and was pleased that her years of trying to make Scott a believer were finally working but what Scott was doing was casing the joint, determining what type of alarm system it had, and if the church was worth the risk.

.....

As soon as Scott's crew closed the paint shop, the white van pulled out.

Once the preacher's sedan pulled off the lot of the church, it passed the white van parked on the street. Scott and his crew were inside the van. With the simple use of a laptop, they were capable of turning off the church alarm system by hacking directly into the security company that monitored the alarm system.

Chapter 11
Vigilante.

The praise of the newspaper articles reinforced Country's conscience-driven sense of obligation. The bold print of the article read: vigilante heroes, shaped and maintained by society. Their unbridled spirit, their passion to achieve a higher standard of morality, to enact true justice above a failed legal system. Is this what America needs to get back on the right path?

After work, Country drove to a corner store in his old neighborhood where he knew some of his homies, also members of his squad, would be hanging out, drinking beer while watching youngsters across the street shooting ball.

Country refused the beer, "Not right now. What's what with Phil Robertson?"

Bo walked out of the store with another six pack, somewhat smirking while shaking his head at Country, "He has been out. Can't make the list."

It wasn't the answer Country wanted. He looked away and redirected his anger at three youngsters who had posted up across the street. They were street servers, petty d'boys, trying to slang the little work they had to come up.

"Get the hell out of here with that shit!"

"Man fuck you! Y'all drinking! How you gonna tell us somethin'?"

Country was done with words. He didn't care about the oncoming cars as he crossed the street.

The youngsters watched, half-amazed, half-scared. "Man, gone on before you make one of us shoot your muthafuckin' ass."

Country's fist hit him directly in the mouth. And before the other two youngsters could react, Country had punched one and kicked the other. They tried to fight back, but Country was too trained and too strong for them. With every punch landed by Country, the agony of pain showed on one of the youngsters' faces. One realized Country was too much to handle, then started searching a nearby bush. He turned around with a gun to see Bo and four others of Country's homies shaking their heads with their guns already drawn.

"Take the ass whipping."

The youngster dropped his gun to be knocked in the bushes by a teeth-rattling punch from Country, who then sat on the youngster's chest, beating him with both fists until Bo and the others pulled him off.

"He's just a kid! Country! That's Boo's baby boy!"

Country had blacked out. He didn't see a child. He saw his enemy. And he would've beaten the youngster to death if his homies hadn't dragged him away.

Chapter 12
Generational Strength.

Annette was in the study of her home, analyzing the recordings of her patients' sessions, when her grandmother entered without knocking,

"I've got us tickets to the stage play The Color Purple. The child who won that television talent show is playing Whoopi. She kind of looks like she could be her daughter."

"Grandma, not tonight."

"It's not tonight. I also got us tickets to the blues concert Betty's son is promoting."

"Devin."

"Yes. Him. He's a fine man. ..."

Annette stopped the tape, restraining her temper while staring at her grandmother, who went on ignoring Annette's grit.

"... I got tickets for Ellis, too."

"Grandma, my evenings are full. I'm not putting you off. My abused women's open house at the gym is three nights a week. I work out the other two. Saturday night is for Ellis and me. You and I can spend Sundays together if that's fine with you."

"Sure, and I can be your assistant at your open house. That's a great service you're providing. I'm ready to go when you're ready."

Annette bit her tongue and just put her things away.

Annette's open house was a mixture of education and a support group.

"What you went through was not your fault. You did what you had to do to stay safe. You have strength and resilience. You are courageous women.

..." After Annette finished her lecture, she opened the mic to others, "....
You are courageous women. Would anyone like to share their experiences?
No one here is alone. I am here for you. We are here for you."

Normally, only two or three women would testify, but it seemed as if no
one would.

"You have already taken the first step by coming out. You are stronger
than you know."

A cute, chubby woman stood. Before she could speak, tears poured from
her eyes, "I have four children. I don't know how we can survive financially
without him."

"I have information about organizations that will shelter you and your
family and help you find a job. Would anyone else like to share their
experience?"

Annette's grandmother realized no one was going to stand, so she stood,

"This is about the strength of my grandmother, who was half white
because her mother had been raped by a white man and became pregnant
with my grand-gran. My gran-gran stood out her entire life, but once she
became grown, she really stood out in our black community, having a Coke
bottle figure with naturally straight hair. A high yellow heifer, as I've also
been called. She had her pick of the fellows, but she fell in love with a
controlling, insecure, powerful black man whose family owned a chicken
farm and a slaughterhouse. To all the others, he was fine, tall, and the best.
To my gran-gran, he became her jailer, torturer, and master. She couldn't
leave the house without him. He made her stop going to college. And when
she spoke out, he beat her. Even though her mother and stepfather and all
of her so-called friends told her she should be happy with a man who could
provide everything she wanted, they didn't understand that she knew her
own worth. She didn't have a support group with someone as smart as my
grandbaby to advise her. ..."

Annette didn't know this part of her family's history, and it showed on her face; the sadness as Annette continued listening to her grandmother.

"... What she had was $15, twin daughters less than a year old, and the same inner voice we all have in us telling us we deserve better. So the very next time he put his hands on her, she gave it to him. You know, they like to fight and fuck. We're grown in here. So she fucked him good. Put him to sleep, then poured gasoline throughout the house, struck a match to it, and moved to L.A. until my mother was 13. Listen to your inner voice. You deserve better than someone beating and abusing you in any way."

At the end of the session, Lulu stepped up to Annette's grandmother with tears. "I'm going through what your grandmother did. I don't know if I have the strength to leave him. I love him. He wasn't always like this. The war did something to him."

Annette's grandmother embraced her, "Baby, you have to love yourself first." Then she led Lulu to Annette.

Chapter 13
Manipulation.

Lulu had received the information, and Annette had given her a free 30-minute one-on-one session. In Annette and Annette's grandmother's presence, Lulu had felt strong enough to make a break from Country but in her car, she weakened; Country hadn't always behaved like he was. In her mind, she knew it was the effects of the war taking a toll, making him sick, twisting his mind. He had been a loving, devoted husband who cherished her. He was sick, and she felt it was her duty as a wife to help him.

There wasn't a light on when Lulu arrived home. But once the living room light did come on, she instantly spotted Country naked, balled up in a corner, weeping.

It seemed sincere, but was a manipulative pity play that appealed to her sympathy.

"I'm sorry. I'm sorry. I can't help it. I can't control my temper. My sessions with Doc are too far apart. ..." This mountain of a man, who had beaten her routinely, moaning and crying, looked like a pathetic wretch.

"... I love you. I'm going to ask Doc for some medication to help me. Please find it in your heart to forgive me? I promise I'm going to do better."

Lulu wiped away his tears, and he kissed her. She pulled back, not expecting him to be so passionate, but he somewhat pulled her back into his kiss. His hand explored under her dress.

"No, babe. Not right here."

"I want you. I want you."

Lulu didn't dare want to make him angry, so she allowed him to make love to her there on the floor of the living room with her clothes on.

Chapter 14
Unraveling.

The DA's case against the Coach was solid from the victim's statement and the character of the victim, even though the community believed the mother was the real culprit. But without damaging evidence against the victim, the odds were that a jury would find the Coach guilty.

I'd flown to New Orleans to the previous community and school of the victim in search of a character flaw, proof she was capable of lying without having a guilty conscience. But I believe I'd gone to prove to myself the Coach wasn't the one capable of such an act. The community and the school were poverty-stricken, nothing like the environment and opportunities the Coach had provided for the victim and her mother. The answers to my questions had the same theme as in Birmingham; all good things about the victim, but the only decent thing said about the mother of the victim was that she loved her daughter. I was directed to the victim's best friend, another young girl who mirrored the victim in appearance. But their attitudes were different.

"... She ain't my friend. She tricked me into doing stuff to her. Nasty stuff. She's nasty for real. She doesn't know how to wash her stuff."

"Are you mad at her?"

"Yeah! She knew I hated this place. She could've made them pick me, too. She just didn't want them to see that my handles are better, and I go to the rack harder. Her shot is better, but mine is good, and I'm making it better. ..." I let her vent. I could see she was hurting and envious of the victim. "... If she were my best friend, ... would you leave your best friend here?"

Reminders of Katrina were still visible. A loud, sexy woman, with the same attitude as the victim's mother, came around the building, cursing at the girl.

"I've told your ass about trying to turn tricks!" The woman eyed me, sizing me up; my appearance, being that I was in a suit and tie, wrapped in my trench coat, made me look extremely out of place.

"Damn! Give us a break. She's making good grades in school. If you arrest her. I don't–"

"I'm not the law. I'm a lawyer investigating–"

"Who are you a lawyer for?"

"Coach Tony."

The woman's disposition changed, "That little she-devil is just like her mama. She did the same damn thing with the department store security guard so her mama and me could steal without worrying about getting caught. She'll do anything for her mama, and Emma will do any damn thing for her."

"Do you know the name of the security guard?"

"Yes. They are my niece and sister. Tell the Coach if he'll get me a job and a house, and put my baby on that team, I'll testify to this and give you the security guard."

I flew home that night. It was hard for me to sleep. I kept feeling the sister's vendetta for the victim and her mother, but it was the damaging evidence needed.

I met with the DA the next morning.

"... I'm advising you to advise this child's mother to drop the case."

I could see the excitement in the DA's eyes over the idea of trying a high-profile case.

"I think a jury will believe this child."

"This child has a bright future ahead of her. This will destroy her life before it's started."

The only future the DA cared about was his own as he smirked at me and left me in the hallway.

Chapter 15
Cross-Examination Of Doubt.

My nights were restless, so that I would get up in the middle of the night and go into another room to read, to get my mind off the case.

Pearl would miss my warmth and awaken, then join me in the den, comforting me by sitting in my lap.

"I hate that I have to do this to this child."

"What if she's telling the truth?"

That was the thing really eating at me. My wife had been raped years earlier, and she'd had to go through hell to prove it herself before the police would even indict the person.

During the following days, I re-interviewed the girls' basketball coach at the elementary school and also the injured boy basketball player, who was in another whirlpool when the Coach supposedly molested the victim. I drilled them both as if I were the prosecutor.

"Does a male coach usually be left alone with female players?"

"Mr. James. Coach has a relationship with all the players. Boys and girls."

"A relationship? In what sense of a relationship?"

"He was concerned!"

"So are you saying the regular rules don't apply to Coach because he has a relationship with the children?"

"Mr. James! You are the Coach's lawyer!"

"I'm asking you the same questions the prosecutor will."

The boy basketball player got just as angry and all crossed up, too.

"I'd gotten out of the whirlpool. But I went back to get my beany I'd left."

"So did or didn't you see Coach next to the whirlpool?"

"He was out of the chair that was next to the whirlpool I was in and was coming toward me."

"How do you know he wasn't coming from beside the whirlpool Ms. Westly was in?"

"Because he wasn't beside it."

"How do you know he wasn't beside her whirlpool while you had gone to the gym, then remembered your beany?"

"I don't know!"

That was the truth, and neither of their testimonies would be any good if they were to take the stand.

....

With only the testimony of the sister and the security guard, Coach's case could be easily won, but I was still feeling uneasy. I met with Emory and Coach in Emory's office. They both were happy about the evidence until they heard the rest of my news.

"I don't want to try this case."

It was like the air went out of the room, and both Emory and Coach were holding their breath.

Emory regained his composure.

"Coach, will you give us a moment, please?"

Emory stood, and Coach did too, while gritting at me,

"You can't do this. He can't quit! It'll look like I'm guilty!"

"Just let me have a word with him."

"I paid you $2 million."

"I know. But you also knew this would be a sensitive issue for him. Give us a moment."

Emory showed Coach out, then returned to his seat and focused on me for a few seconds, "Is he guilty?"

"I don't know."

"You only take cases you can win. You've won this one already."

"I only take cases I believe are worth winning! I'm not sure he's innocent!"

"You just said you're not certain he's guilty. I'm not telling him. Tell him yourself."

Emory buzzed his secretary.

"Send him back in."

Coach entered, begging, "Don't turn your back on me. I helped you build your confidence. I believed in your flicked shot. I pushed you."

He was partially right; he helped build my confidence, but he was minor compared to my mother.

"I love those kids. I know her mother is using her. I'm 65. I don't want to go to prison. Not as a pedophile."

I did owe him a lot, so I agreed to stay on.

Chapter 16
Dark Secrets.

Three more churches had been burned to the ground. Pressure was being applied from all angles: the media, the Bible-Belt groups, and the brass, and the weight of it all landed on the shoulders of Ellis Collins.

Ellis Collins thought he'd caught a break after days of going over the pictures from the traffic light cameras. The same make of van but in several different colors, had been identified coming and leaving the vicinity of the churches, which coincided with the times of the burnings, but once the pictures were blown up, the windows of the van were too darkly tinted to identify who or how many were inside, and its license plate was different for each burning.

None of the plates were registered to a van, but did belong to vehicles owned by UAB students.

Next, Ellis Collins did the most sensible thing: He put stakeouts on the most vulnerable churches and the biggest ones, just in case the suspects were doing it to make a statement.

It was cold and raining, and Ellis Collins wished he were in his bed or at least in Annette's. Then, through his binoculars, he saw the light of a cell phone in a car half a block up, parked across from the church's parking lot. He got out into the pouring rain to investigate closer. He was soaked, but he could make out that it was a woman in the car. Further adjusting the binoculars, he saw it was the female journalist Connie Cox.

Connie Cox was drinking from her cup of latté, focused on AME when Ellis Collins opened the passenger side door and sat in her car.

"Police business can be really dangerous." Ellis Collins knew he'd caught her off guard.

Surprise and fear made Connie Cox scream and drop her cup of coffee into her lap. She covered her embarrassment by pretending it was the heat of the coffee that had spilled all over her.

"Goddamnit! Get the hell out of my car! Get out!"

With a satisfying smirk, Ellis Collins stepped out into the pouring rain, but paused, staring back inside the car at her,

"We don't know what we're dealing with. I suggest you write about this one from what I report to you."

Chapter 17
More but Better.

AME would've been the ultimate lick. Scott had it all planned out. The rainy weather was ideal. As a safety precaution, he'd driven ahead of the van in Candy's car to case out the mega church. Everything seemed perfect. Scott was about to call the van in when he noticed a man step out of a car into the rain. It was hard for Scott to determine if it was Ellis Collins in the pouring rain, but Scott didn't chance it.

Instead, Scott drove to a church in Pelham, Alabama, a small city on the edge of Birmingham. The church was a gold mine of gold artifacts. The silence of Scott's crew at the paint shop told them all knew they'd been lucky that night.

"This should do it," Scott really did want to be done. "But I'm not sure what YG's asking." But he knew they all would do whatever it took to bring their dreams to life.

Scott's apartment was pitch black and silent. Sadie and Candy both seemed to be sound asleep when he entered the bedroom. There was an old rocking chair in the corner of the room. It had been there since Sadie's collie days, and they'd used it to rock her to sleep.

Instead of doing anything to wake them, Scott sat in the chair and stared at his family, his future. He wanted better, more for them.

Scott's eyes adjusted to the dark, and he realized Candy was staring back at him. She slid out of bed without waking Sadie, then sat in Scott's lap.

"Aren't you working double shifts tomorrow?"

"You know I can't sleep until you make it home. What's on your mind?"

"You two deserve better."

"Our time is coming soon. We're going to be rich and famous and be able to afford to have as many children as we want."

Candy kissed him, then stood. Her sexy little nightie rose as she mounted him. Her long legs hung out of the back of the chair as they rocked and groaned with her riding him while his face was buried between her breasts.

"I'll do anything for you. I love you."

Candy's mouth covered his. Her tongue deep into his mouth as their bodies melted into one.

Chapter 18
Crossfire.

Ellis Collins was scanning the articles on the USA Today's website, then stopped and completely read Connie Cox's article about a church being burned to the ground, while the lead detective stated he couldn't believe it was homegrown terrorists or even an act of racism.

Ellis Collins knew the shit would hit the fan once he got to the station. And sure enough, the captain stood in the doorway of her office with a newspaper balled up in her hand. Her facial expression and the fact she was mad enough that sound couldn't come out of her mouth told her disposition as she gestured with the newspaper for him to come to her office.

"Close my door. Don't sit down. Tell me you were not giving this interview while a church was being burned to the ground."

He couldn't deny it, so he remained silent.

"At least tell me she misquoted you."

Again, he remained silent, fighting the urge to speak out.

"Are you trying to serve her your head on a silver platter?"

"The damn church wasn't even in our jurisdiction! Nothing we've found points to terrorism or racism."

"What have you found that points to anything?"

"We know the make and model of the van. We knew the suspect or suspects must work near or attend UAB," Ellis Collins read in her face. It wasn't enough.

"Damn Paris. It's not like fingerprints are being left. These are the only two things connecting the crimes."

"You do realize your neck isn't the only one on the line. I don't like her, but I like my job. I don't give a damn if they're terrorists or students do something to catch whoever the hell this is!"

Ellis Collins and his team went back to step one, the churches, then checked every possible reason someone would burn a building.

Ellis Collins needed a distraction from police work. Ebony had come home for the weekend from college, but had spent most of her time with her girlfriends.

He finally cornered his daughter at breakfast.

"... She's important to me, and since you're–"

"Dad, you have my blessings if you want to marry Annette. I like her and the way she treats you and Grandma."

"Be at brunch."

"I will. Don't wait up tonight." Then she quickly kissed his cheek before going to her room.

Ellis Collins realized his daughter still had on her party clothes, meaning she was just getting home.

Brunch was at Ira's restaurant. Live Jazz music was played, and mimosas were constantly being refilled.

Annette's grandmother loved the atmosphere. "This would be a nice place to get married."

Annette made light of it. "Grandma, who are you about to marry? Have I met him?" holding back her laughter while smiling at Ebony and Ellis Collins' mother-in-law. She saw Ebony's eyes dart to her father as if signaling him to say something.

But Ellis Collins only drank his orange juice.

Annette's grandmother took over the conversation again, "Why don't you go ahead and become a lawyer? A lawyer is a safe job to raise a family before my grandbaby becomes too mature for children. What do you think, Mae?"

Ellis Collins' mother-in-law somewhat agreed. "You have been thinking about a lot of things. I agree that it's no time better to do them than the present time."

Annette saw Ellis Collins going into the inside pocket of his jacket.

"If you're not ready, don't allow anyone to rush you."

"I'm more than ready to do this. You have helped me out of the deepest hole I've ever faced. You've learned all of my dark secrets and haven't run away. I never thought I could love again, but I can, and it's because of you. I love you and want you to be my wife. Will you marry me?"

All four of the ladies at the table had tears in their eyes and smiles on their faces.

"Yes! Yes!"

Ellis Collins placed the huge diamond ring on Annette's finger, and the entire restaurant applauded.

Chapter 19
Middleman.

Looting the churches was the easy part. Finding someone trustworthy to buy it and keep their mouth shut was the extremely difficult part. Scott had been introduced to a brother who owned a jewelry store, Ali, who portrayed himself as a Nigerian with a broad African accent.

Since the price of gold was close to $2,000 an ounce, greed had made Ali, Scott's partner. His shop was in Western Hill's Mall. Scott and his crew were with Ali in the storage area of the shop with the five duffel bags of gold items stolen from the church.

"... Look man, we had a deal. Keep trying to rob us, and we'll come back and rob your ass for real."

"Here. You Americans always complain. Cry, cry, cry."

"Sounds like you're doing all the damn crying. Thank you." Scott cuffed one of the diamond rings that Ali had on the mounting device. "Every penny better be there."

The bedroom light was on when Scott entered his apartment. Candy was up reading her Bible.

"You're home early?"

"Yes, I am." Scott took her hand and removed the Cracker-Jack wedding ring, then replaced it with the one he'd stolen from Ali.

Candy became excited, then suspicious.

"Tell me you're not selling drugs."

"I'm not."

"What are you doing?"

"Making your dreams come true."

"You did that when you came into my life." ....

Scott had made the arrangements and flown YG into Birmingham to spit on Candy's track. They were at the studio recording. The song was smooth, sensual, and sultry mood music. YG had the perfect flow and delivery for it, but his content lacked depth.

Scott instantly stopped playing the keyboard. "Whoa! Whoa Bro! This track is for more than kids."

"What! This is fire!"

"That shit's childish. Bro, this is an instant classic without you."

"Why the fuck do you need me?"

Scott did need him and had paid him. "Because you're that dude who can take it beyond that. This song is meant to touch virgins to grandmas using walkers. I want your words to make every woman cream."

"You write it, and I'll spit them."

"Bro, I've already paid you –"

"For this. It took three days to write this." This was coming from one of the supposedly best rappers to ever live, and who never wrote down anything. Scott didn't lose it. He read over YG's lyrics, then gave them back to him.

"Y'all take a break. Go get a bite to eat."

Candy recognized the anguish in Scott's expression. "What are you about to do?" Her touch brought a smile to his face.

"Save the day, like always. I'll be done by the time y'all get back."

The others all left but YG. He stayed in the booth, looking over Scott's shoulder nodding his head while reading the lyrics aloud. Every once in a while, Scott would have to stop YG and define and pronounce a word. YG didn't get mad; instead, when Scott finished and ripped the page out of his notebook, YG was so impressed.

"How much will it take for you to sell me your lyrics book?"

"It's not for sale. ... But what we can do is I'll write you two songs if you spit on two of Candy's tracks and one on my group."

"As long as you write the lyrics for the songs also."

"Cool." Scott took out a blunt and sparked it, which he and YG were still burning when everyone returned.

"I see why you wanted to get rid of us." Big CJ took the blunt. "Are we ready to jam or what?"

"Let's make it happen captain."

Everyone was stoked over the strength of the two songs, plus Candy's CD was complete.

Candy was hugging Scott when YG went into his backpack and dropped 60 racks on the keyboard in front of Scott.

"I want two more songs before my flight in the morning."

Candy kissed Scott, then released him.

"I'm going to pick up Sadie from your mom's. Don't be forever."

Big CJ and the other guys took YG out on the city, while Scott stayed at the studio writing.

Chapter 20
Blood and Rubies.

The fake police jump-out unit had struck again. The home was a bloody massacre. Bodies were throughout the house. Ellis Collins stepped over puddles of blood that led to one of the city's most notorious drug lord's body.

A single shot had ended his life. The bullet hole was in the center of his forehead and had blown off the back of his head.

Ellis Collins scanned the body, the position the body laid, then saw the bullet hole in the window. Half a block away, he saw a telegram pole and imagined the sniper sitting there staring back through the scope of his rifle, watching in satisfaction.

"Huh."

Large amounts of drugs were throughout the house, and expensive Gotti jewelry was still on the bodies. But not a penny or bullet casing could be found.

One piece of jewelry stood out, caught Ellis Collins' attention. He really didn't give a damn about the dead drug dealers, but the heavy gold jewelry had him thinking. So he took the pieces off the body.

"Write it up as evidence." Answering the stare of one of the members of the forensic team.

The pieces of jewelry were custom-made; Ellis Collins had no doubt about it. It was the size of the rubies in the pieces that made him suspicious. They looked identical to the rubies in a cross that had been in one of the churches burned to the ground. The pictures from the insurance company didn't exactly confirm it but it could've been them.

Ellis Collins went with his hunch and went to all the local jewelers, showing them the pieces.

"I sell jewelry. Don't buy it."

"Is this your work?"

"No. That's messy. Rushed. That's Ali's."

After two more jewelers also identified the pieces as Ali's work, Ellis Collins paid Ali's Jewelry store a visit.

"Yes. I made those. Beautiful work, isn't it?"

"How?"

"I buy old jewelry and make my own modes."

"Can we see how?"

"I'm busy. ..." Seeing how his customers were entering the store, then immediately leaving once they recognized Ellis Collins and the two other detectives with him.

"... I'm sorry, I can't help you with the murder of my customers. My customers are from all walks of life."

The store sold custom-made jewelry for ballas, and d'boys, and Ellis Collins knew it.

Chapter 21
Behavioral Patterns.

Annette was at the police station, profiling the behavioral patterns of the fake jump out unit,

"... They're well trained and highly efficient as a group. They are killers who see themselves as heroes. They are nearly conscience-free. Not held back by guilt when trying to complete their mission. They are not underachievers. They have no nagging voice in their heads that prevents them from doing everything and anything they have to do to succeed."

Annette noticed how once the captain saw Ellis Collins entering the room, she aggressively got up and led him out into the hallway.

"To them, this is evil versus good."

In the hallway, the captain was barking at Ellis Collins.

"... About the church burnings. It's been two weeks since the last one! If they stop, you may never find them."

"I put in a request for a search warrant that was refused!"

"It was a jewelry store! What in the hell does it have to do with squat?"

"I think everything!"

The captain gained her composure, absorbing what he'd said.

"Well, do what you have to, to get it!" Then she walked off, passing Annette, who was a few feet away waiting.

"Don't distract him."

Annette was just as frustrated as Ellis Collins. Once he embraced her, she whispered in his ear.

"I need a quickie."

"Me too. But I don't have time."

"I need to release the stress from my grandmother, or I'm going to kill her."

Ellis Collins tried to keep from laughing at her.

"It's not funny!"

Ellis Collins took Annette into his arms and kissed her forehead.

"She's just trying to be a part of your life."

"Why mine? Why not one of my sisters?"

"She sees more of herself in you. You should be grateful to be able to spend time with her. I've got to go."

Annette was at her office, scarfing down a chicken Caesar salad when her receptionist buzzed.

"Your grandmother is on line one, and your one o'clock is here already."

Annette picked up the phone and impatiently listened.

"Grandma, I'm eating lunch now. … I can't. I have sessions. … Grandma. … Grandma, I'll see you tonight. Bye. Bye Grandma. I'm hanging up. Bye-bye."

She hung up, then stared up at the ceiling before silently screaming.

Annette finished the last of her salad, then pressed the button on her intercom.

"Send Sergeant Madison in, please."

Country entered anxiously, fidgeting as he sat on the couch.

"You're early. Is there an emergency issue we need to discuss?"

"I'm swamped at work. I was hoping you would be able to see me early because I've got to get back."

"Okay, where would you like to begin?"

Annette watched how his suspicious eyes scanned the room, somewhat inventorying the office for anything new or out of place.

"I, I, I can't understand how people don't get the importance of commitment. When you say you're going to do something, do it! At least give it your all to try to do it! You have to be loyal to something! Especially your purpose. A man ain't nothing without a purpose!"

Annette sensed his eyes were evaluating her, waiting for her reply.

"A lot of people haven't learned their purpose."

"Then they need discipline."

"What's your purpose?"

Country's posture became erect, and his tone and his words clear and precise.

"To serve God. To serve my family, my community, my city, my state, my country!"

"War allows you to do that?"

"Yes! War allows me to do what's needed!"

Country's watch alarmed, and he stood, tense, on edge but didn't move.

"Are you sure you don't want to finish this session?"

"Next week, Doc. I'm swamped at work."

Chapter 22
Pride or Justice.

Ellis Collins had been constantly calling Judge Wallace the entire day to be blown off by the judge's aide. Finally, Ellis Collins made up his mind to personally go to the court building, but the Judge had left for the day.

Judge Wallace and Ellis Collins were both supposedly out to serve justice, but personally, they were mortal enemies due to the fact that Ellis Collins had headed the case that led to the judge's son committing suicide.

Ellis Collins entered the massive estate of the judge's home. A six-year-old child answered the door.

"Is the judge in?"

She didn't know any better and nodded before allowing Ellis Collins inside the home. "They're in the study."

Ellis Collins smiled at her as she took his hand and led the way. The interior of the home was more extravagant than the outside. The little girl drew open the divided doors. In the study sat three heavyset elderly, distinguished men: the judge, the ex-mayor, and the ex-chief of police. They were now openly business partners, and each had some sort of bone to pick with Ellis Collins.

The judge stood, going for a shotgun mounted on the wall. "What in the hell are you doing in my home!"

"I'm here on police business." Ellis Collins stood his ground while blatantly holding out his arms so all could see him slowly remove the strap holding his 9 millimeter in its mount on his side.

"I put in a request for a search warrant weeks ago. I need that search warrant to catch the suspects of the church burnings."

The ex-mayor stood and stepped toward Ellis Collins with a smirk. "I suggest you leave. Or we might have another hate crime on our hands."

Ellis Collins was focused on the judge who had the rifle in his hand, but was looking for the shells to load it.

"They may be hate crimes or not, but the search warrant may link us to items stolen from the churches." He extended a folder toward the judge who had found the box of shells he'd been searching for.

"These are the insurance companies' invoices of the artifacts stolen from all the churches, which have a combined total of over $3 million. Hate could be the motive, but money has always been a great incentive."

The judge closed the barrel of the shotgun and raised it. His expression showed how badly he wanted to pull the trigger, but instead, he put the gun down.

.....

The mall was closed; even the employees had cleaned up and gone. But music echoed from the east wing, Ali's jewelry store. The security guard used a master key to open the gate to enter the store for Ellis Collins and four police officers.

The music was coming from the storage area where a light shone under the closed door. Ali was in the back room with an oxyacetylene torch, melting down a two-foot gold cross encrusted with giant rubies. Ali didn't know they were in the room until the fire of the torch went out.

Ellis Collins smirked at Ali and nodded like, "Yeah, we've got you."

Ali dropped his foreign accent. "I buy old jewelry. I don't know where it came from. I don't ask."

"I can tell where it came from, but I want you to tell me who sold it to you."

"I can't do that! It'll put me out of business if I rat on a customer!"

Ellis Collins was searching around the area while holding the conversation. The cross was the last piece in the duffel bag.

"Hate crimes carry 25 years to life. Fed-time. I'm pretty sure your business will be gone under by then."

"Damn man! The only name I know him by is Milk."

"Cuff him."

"Wait! This is my livelihood. ... He's a white rapper. That's all I know."

"Thank you. Cuff him."

Ali seemed to be about to cry as the officer put Ali's hands behind his back, "I've told you what you wanted!"

"You're still getting arrested for buying stolen property. Just not a hate crime."

Chapter 23
Bingo.

To appease her grandmother, Annette had skipped her workout to take her grandmother to play bingo, which wasn't officially bingo but a charity hosted by me that used bingo to pick the winners of consolation prizes for contributing to the cause. Annette loved it, but her grandmother hated it,

"I told you I don't like smelling old folks. It smells like people are about to die in here." Her mood quickly changed once the place became packed with young women and men."

"Betsy's son is so fine! But he has a ring on. I'm not breaking up any more happy homes. I've had my fill of that. But this one is ripe for the picking."

Annette's grandmother batted her eyes at Ira, one of Birmingham's most debonair older single gentlemen who was passing with me. Ira happily stopped to flirt with her.

"You must be Annette's sister? I thought I had met them all. I'm Ira."

"You're a little too old for me, but you're fine so I'll make an exception as long as you're capable of handling your business."

Annette was so embarrassed that she covered her face in disbelief. But Ira and her grandmother truly enjoyed flirting, and Annette enjoyed seeing her grandmother smiling and laughing.

The night had gone well, and Annette was proud of herself for finding something she and her grandmother could enjoy together.

Annette had dressed for bed, then grabbed her e-tablet and logged onto her website to update her Twitter account and to check her blog questions.

Annette immediately started screaming.

Her grandmother ran into the room with her taser.

"What! What is the problem child?"

"You have updated my blog! And answered my viewers' questions!"

"Yeah. You were taking so long so I–"

"People don't need to hear feel-good stories! They need to be made aware of the true behavioral tendency that is the cause of the act!"

Annette's grandmother quickly lost her humble apologetic tone and became stern.

"Don't forget, young lady, I also have a doctorate in psychology!"

"But this is my space, my comfort zone. Don't crowd the last little piece of me, please!"

Her statement struck like a knife. The pain showed in her grandmother's posture, her tone.

"Why did you invite me to stay if I'm crowding you?"

The sight of sadness on her grandmother's face humbled Annette and softened her anger.

"I love you, Grandma, and have always loved learning from you but we have to give each other a little space. Our own privacy."

Chapter 24
Milk.

Ellis Collins had caught the break he needed, or at least he thought so.

He'd gone to all the multicultural hip hop spots asking for Milk the rapper.

Quite a few people knew Milk. "Yeah, but I don't know his real name."

It was frustrating, but it didn't deter Ellis Collins. As he was about to leave the last club, the Hot's music on wheels van pulled up.

Hot's was a hustler with a peddler's license to sell CDs, DVDs, and anything else he thought dealt with hip-hop.

"Hot's my man!"

"Damn. Look, man, I've straightened up my life. You're –"

"This has nothing to do with you. Do you know of a rapper named Milk?"

"Yeah. Good kid. He and his crew. Here …" He extended a copy of Milk's group CD. "$20. You can learn a lot about Milk. Listen to this."

Ellis Collins was somewhat stunned by the title. "Milk Chocolate?"

"He thinks he's black. All four carry it that way. They're good kids. Smoke too much bud, but smart kids. And damn good rappers." He could see Ellis Collins mentally absorbing everything he said. "These are good kids, remember this, if they're into something they shouldn't be."

"Do you know where I can find them?"

Hot's started ringing up CDs and a few T-shirts, "Your total is $230."

Ellis Collins angrily took out all of the remaining cash from his wallet and handed it to Hots.

"They all work at the paint stop on the Southside, and are all full-time students on band scholarships at UAB."

Instead of Hots passing the bag of items to Ellis Collins, he started to put them back.

"Man, if you don't give me my shit!"

The first thing Ellis Collins did the next morning was go to the paint shop.

The CD cover was wallpapered on the van parked out front. The tire treads matched those left at the churches. Ellis Collins was picking at a corner of the cover off the van when Slim, the owner of the shop, stepped outside.

"You're interested in being a billboard on wheels?"

"How long would it take?"

"Less than an hour, but I won't be able to do it until next week."

"Why?"

"My employees who do it are off rehearsing for a showcase or something."

"You mean Milk and his group?"

"Yeah. They're putting on a show at the old French quarters tonight. Made me promise to support them. I hate that shit, but they work so hard for me. I've got to go."

"I'll probably see you there."

At the station, an FBI agent sat in the captain's office, cocky ass Agent McWilliams. The captain's eyes met Ellis Collins as he stood in her doorway.

"Detective Collins, c'mon in. This is Agent McWilliams. He will be assisting you."

“On what?”

“The hate crimes and the vigilante killings.”

“Not to assist but to supervise the cases.” Agent McWilliams arrogantly asserted his command.

“We haven’t determined that they are hate crimes. … I know the whereabouts of the suspects of the church burnings. The evidence I used to locate these suspects has nothing to do with crimes of hate.”

The media attention was the cause of Agent McWilliams being sent to Birmingham. “This is a federal case now.” He wasn’t about to miss being in the spotlight.

Chapter 25
Showcase.

Scott had tried to divide the $60,000 with the guys, but they agreed to use the money on more promotion and studio time the plan which Scott had lined up; showcasing at a nightclub in all the major black cities throughout the south. Once they were done with those, they were to hit the historically Black colleges and Universities. Birmingham was their home and starting point.

It was the night of their first showcase. For a dead night, the French Quarter's club was packed. The showcase gave the youth of the city something to do, plus Scott had used a large sum to get Candy and YG's single in rotation on the radio. The song was hot, and the people had come out to hear more.

The stage was set up, but Scott and his crew were in the back room, burning some weed, taking the edge off before they opened up for Candy. A SWAT team stormed the club. People were in shock seeing the automatic weapons and the intensified movement of the team. It was like a video game with the infra-red dots included.

Neither Scott nor the others resisted but were roughed up anyway and dragged out of the club.

Ellis Collins noticed Candy and the backup singers approaching, screaming and crying, and then stepped in front of them.

"What have they done! They're not resisting! Y'all don't have to do them like that!"

"I'm advising you to stay back."

"That's my husband, they're doing like that! ..." The news shocked Ellis Collins, but he managed to block their way and grab Candy.

"... Stop them! They're going to kill them!"

Ellis Collins quickly stepped to Agent McWilliams, "There's a lot of cell phone in here with cameras. You are the head of this. Not me."

"Get them out of here!"

Most of the law enforcement in Birmingham were Black, and since the media had painted a picture of the suspects as racists leftover from the Sixties so the black enforcement officers seemed to all have personal vendettas against Scott and his crew.

At the county jail in the holding cell, the sheriffs gave Scott and his crew lice-infested clothes and blankets, which they felt the effects of the very next morning. When Scott complained, the sheriffs shaved their heads and hosed them down like during the Sixties, then doused them with powder.

Television crews and thousands of spectators were gathered mob-style outside the county jail and in front of the court building. The sheriffs had placed bulletproof vests on Scott and his crew as they transported them to their arraignment. Scott and his crew resembled the skinheads the papers and television news had painted in the minds of the world.

Their public defender was a young brother who seemed scared of them and the case itself. He didn't say a word to them or for them, not even when they were charged with 13 hate crimes, which each one of them denied with conviction since they were actually telling the truth. Scott knew there was no way they could be made to be racists. He'd thought it all the way through from the beginning. All they had to do was take it to court if they got caught.

Chapter 26
Unity.

Neither Scott nor any of the others had done time, so there was a flaw in his plan. He hadn't anticipated the reaction from the other inmates. When Scott and his crew returned from court, they were placed in a dorm with 120 inmates.

Scott and his crew stood as one, like always. The brothers were mugging, not knowing how to handle them, especially after Scott had shaken off a white boy with a huge swastika tattooed on his neck.

Walt B, a D'boy who had tried to sign Scott, was in the dorm. He'd been sentenced to 15 years but was waiting to be shipped out. Walt B. recognized Scott and stepped in and took Scott aside.

"Come clean, homie."

"They were licks to pay for studio time and YG. Only two of the 13 churches had black preachers. The media twisted shit to move papers and to get ratings."

Walt B didn't believe Scott was racist from the beginning, "Give a concert or something. Let the brothers feel y'all. Y'all rockin' the hell out of that skinhead look."

Scott didn't want anyone to think they were bowing down to anyone or anything, but he understood the situation, "The only hate we have is of the system and ignorant fuckas. We're about to give you the Soul of Milk Chocolate in one voice! But don't get it twisted, because if y'all bring it we're gonna handle it!"

Scott and his crew rocked the dorm until the angry ass sheriffs racked everyone down. But that didn't stop Scott's crew from taking requests from blacks and whites throughout the night singing and rapping. It wasn't about color. It was hip-hop, their culture that was what Scott and his crew saw.

Chapter 27
Unlikely.

I stepped out of my office to see Emory and Candy with her daughter on her hip, headed in my direction.

"Mr. James, this is Candace Horrid, the wife of Scott Horrid, who has been charged with the hate crimes of burning churches. She has obtained our services." Candy had continued promoting her music at small venues, following Scott's plan, but was using the door money to pay for my services.

Emory had accepted because of the publicity he knew the firm would get. "One second, Miss." I took Emory into my office, leaving Candy in the hallway, "Did you make me a partner to try every circus act that comes through here?"

"I figured you would be pleased with this one, seeing how ironic it is. And it has merit. Wait until you read the discovery and hear her story." Emory was right; they were silly charges, and her story was heartfelt.

I met with the overzealous DA, and he laughed at me when I suggested, "Offer the boys a deal, or they will walk."

The DA was another glory hound, hungry for a big case. He wasn't about to let it get away. I wasn't in a playing mood. He was more interested in his career than in justice.

"Fine."

Pearl and I were on a dinner date with Ellis Collins and Annette. The restaurant was upscale and trendy. Ellis Collins and I both tried to stay off the subjects of the cases. I could tell both ladies needed the evening out and had taken plenty of time and attention in preparing for the evening. They both looked gorgeous.

Once they went to the restroom, Ellis Collins and I used the opportunity to see where we stood on the cases.

"You know these hate crime charges are bogus?"

Ellis Collins' smirk answered mine. "Yeah. They're some smart young criminals who probably outsmarted themselves."

"Yeah, but they don't deserve 25 to life."

"Nope, I can't say they do. But they don't deserve to walk."

"I can't say they do, but they will under hate crimes."

The ladies returned, and both immediately lost their smiles.

"You promised!"

"What! We're just catching up. Nupe, when y'all going to Atlanta to check up on Ebony? We can make it a trip to see AJ play, too."

"Soon, very soon. Nupe ..."

Both ladies sat and started back to enjoy themselves, talking about the wedding.

Jury selection for the Coach's trial was more like checkers than chess.

Regardless of who I chose, the DA struck them for no apparent reason except that I wanted them.

"Your Honor, let the DA make his selections first, please." The judge was just as frustrated, so she agreed.

The DA's first question to an older man showed he wasn't quite a moron.

"Did you like seeing the defendant playing basketball?"

I couldn't allow him to get an answer.

"Your Honor! My client is a pro basketball Hall-of-Famer. Everyone in Alabama knows him. I'm going to strike them if they say no. This could only take about twenty years."

"It's due process, your honor."

The judge allowed him to proceed. It was truly a frustrating process, and on top of that, when I was about to strike a big-breasted woman, Coach touched my hand and shook his head.

"Keep her."

"What? She was abused when she was 12 by her uncle."

"Keep her."

I saw the infatuation in his eyes. His direct gaze was inescapable. He was fixated on the woman's breasts, so something in me was happy to go against my better judgment, and I allowed her to stay on as a juror.

Chapter 28
The Truth.

Scott and the others were pulled out of the dorm and escorted to a visiting room. The peach fuzz amount of hair that had grown back on their heads had them looking like psycho-neo-Nazis.

After the formalities, I was straightforward with them, "You're looking at a life sentence. I can beat the hate crime charges, but 13 counts of arson can be as high as 30 years."

Scott was the spokesperson for them: "No one saw us."

"Ali gave you up, and they have artifacts from the last church. Plus, your tire prints were at all the scenes."

"Those are standard-issued. That means nothing. Ali's statement only means we gave him stolen goods."

At that point, I was taken aback at how well thought-out the crime they'd committed.

"Why did you burn the churches? Don't lie to me, or I will walk."

"We were just covering the fact that we were stealing. We're thieves not racists."

I had somewhat of an understanding of them, which was why I'd visited them. "I'll be in touch."

It was three days before the Coach's trial. I hand-delivered Annette's psychological evaluation of the victim, Doc's physical examination of the injury that had landed the victim in the whirlpool, along with the affidavits of the victim's aunt and the security guard, to the DA proceeding over the Coach's trial.

"When you finish reading these, call me."

I didn't have time to wait. I'd scheduled a meeting with the overzealous DA, Agent McWilliams, and Ellis Collins pertaining to the hate crimes case. Everyone seemed annoyed except Ellis Collins.

"... five years max with 18 months off for the drug program, or we crank up the jury."

The DA was also a cocky, self-righteous bastard. "We have a witness and physical evidence."

"You have a convicted felon and prints of a standard issue tire. The facts are Scott Horrid is married to an African American woman and has a mixed child, and the others all date black women and have a CD denouncing all types of hate." I left the CD with them.

The DA was on my cell before I made it to my car.

Chapter 29
Dilemma.

Since Ellis Collins' part in the church burning case was done, he focused all his energy on the investigation of the fake jump-out unit. The bad part was that McWilliams was also investigating the case.

"The robbers are not cops!"

"How are you so sure?"

"Their financial debt!" Ellis Collins had gone through every officer's personal finances.

"... If they had large sums of cash, why do their checking account or savings accounts equal only a fourth of their monthly salary?"

McWilliams wasn't half the detective Ellis Collins was. McWilliams didn't see the connection,

"What the hell does that mean?"

"If they had the cash, why would they spend their salary?"

"What about the police units and the missing armor gear?"

"Auctions! We sell the damn things! And the squad doesn't turn in their equipment."

Ellis Collins was trying to shake McWilliams, who continued following him through the station.

"What about the high-powered artillery?"

"If the inventory of our armory shows anything missing, then it could imply one of ours, but as of yet, nothing is missing according to the invoices."

Once Ellis Collins had gotten away from McWilliams, he turned into another argument with the DA, who was the prosecutor of the Horrid case. Ellis Collins simply walked off. He'd had it with dealing with incompetent people.

"I'm rolling the dice with the Horrid case. No deal. I might need–"

The media was pressing for a lynching, and he'd bent, caved in.

"I won't give false testimony. I'm advising you not to put me on the stand."

"Agent McWilliams will do fine."

"Fine!"

This was the part of law enforcement that Ellis Collins didn't like, which made him think about leaving law enforcement.

Chapter 30
Consequences.

The Coach and Emory were in my office. Coach was being adamant about going to trial, which I was totally against.

"You don't have to ruin this child's life."

Coach adopted a posture of righteous indignation and became angry. "She tried to destroy mine!"

"If he's trying to press on with this, I'm done."

Emory could tell by my expression that I was serious, "Trial isn't a 100 percent guaranteed. Jurors can be very sentimental. I agree with my partner. You should take your victory."

Two hours later, Coach and I met with the prosecutor, the victim, and her mother. I was discussing the reasons for the case to be dropped. The victim's eyes were angrily glued on the Coach. She shed soundless tears, but her expression would have never suggested she was crying.

"He did! He did! I'm not lying, ma! I'm not!"

The mother became frantic, tears and spit flew as she spoke.

"This muthafuckin' monster ain't getting away with touching my baby! I swear to God muthafucka, you're gonna pay for this!"

Coach sat there with a shit-eating grin, ignoring the mother, but staring at the young girl. Then he looked at me, right in my eyes, and it was as if I'd never met him before in my life. And I realized all of a sudden that in his mind, this was some kind of control game. And I had lost big time. He'd made it his business to know how I could be manipulated and used. I wanted to beat his ass myself.

Why would a person like that do such a horrible thing? Why would a normal-looking person, a person who looked just like us, a person entrusted with authority, commit such a horrible act of touching a child?

I didn't want the victim to think she was to blame. I didn't want her to lose faith, partially or completely, in herself.

"You might not understand this now, but some battles must be lost to win the war. But remember this, if it's his nature, you two have made it so no other girls will get touched by–"

The prosecutor's jaw dropped in shock.

"You think he's guilty!"

I did, but it didn't matter at that point.

"Even if he is, he is a leader of the community, a Hall of Famer. He's like a grandfather to thousands. ... I think if you don't drop this case, your career will be destroyed for seeking to advance it by going after a celebrity. Say it is to not further scar and emotionally damage the young ego of the victim. All charges have to be dropped and dismissed. Also, a hush contract will have to be signed."

"I ain't signing a damn thing!" The mother couldn't control her outburst.

"Yes, you are. Or I'll press charges against you for attempted blackmail."

Once the papers were signed and the coach and I were outside the federal building, I wanted to put as much distance between the coach and me as possible.

"Devin, I just–"

"Don't touch me! Don't put your filthy hands on me! All legally binding contracts between the firm and you are exhausted, and we will no longer represent you!"

Chapter 31
Tactical.

Annette was in the study on her laptop, going over the schematics of the robbers, when Ellis Collins entered with takeout food.

"Where's grandma?"

"She just left, going shopping."

Ellis Collins immediately started undressing while staring at the charts.

"These are too tactical of kill strikes for the unit to be untrained."

"That doesn't mean they're policemen." This was the consensus around the city.

"A military mind designed these attacks. All the areas of escape were covered. Plus shots guided everyone who was inside to here for the kill."

Annette stared at him, standing there only in his boxers and socks, so he poked the cart to get her attention and her professional input. She examined the charts closer then stared up at Ellis Collins, who seemed frustrated because she didn't see what he saw.

"The death blows are from a sniper through the window for everyone!"

Slowly, her thought came to her. "They think they're heroes. So what kind of heroes do you think?"

"War heroes!" Ellis Collins started picking up his clothes.

"Hell naw! I need this, too!" Annette snatched the clothes out of the hands of Ellis Collins

.

Chapter 32
Predators.

Country was at work, mopping the hallway, when he overheard and saw the tears of the victim in Coach's case, crying to her mother and the DA.

"He touched me. I'm not lying!"

The prosecutor ignored her plea and walked off without a care, while the mother wiped away the girl's tears.

"Don't worry, don't worry, somehow he'll get his issue. I promise you. C'mon, you've still got practice."

"I don't want to."

"Shit, you love basketball. You ain't gonna let this muthafucka take that from you. Let's go. We're stronger than this and his bitch-ass!"

Some might not have agreed with her child-rearing method, but for the circumstances, she was the right type of mother.

Country held the door open for them, seeing them as the unprotected underdogs.

Coach was sitting on the hood of his car, gloating, staring at the mother and daughter as they passed.

The mother snapped. "What the fuck are your old punk ass looking at?"

"You got 30 days to get your trifling asses out of my house."

"My baby is still the star of the team!"

"For now." Coach thought he'd gotten the best of them, laughing to himself as he got into his car.

Unknown to Coach was that when he drove off, Country was in a car trailing behind him.

Country was coy and patient, stalking as if the Coach was his prey.

Coach stopped at a car wash, chatted with a shady-looking youngster who left, but returned with two young girls before the Coach's car was finished being hand-detailed. The Coach made a head gesture toward the youngest-looking of the two girls. She looked no older than 13, barely developed. She got into his car while Coach gave the guy a knot of cash.

Country followed the Coach for a couple of blocks to an out-of-the-way motel, where the coach and the child went into a room. Within twenty minutes, the coach was on the move again, and so was Country.

The coach's destination was the Oak Mountain area to a lake cabin.

Country waited until the lights in the cabin went out before he even got out of his car. He crept toward the cabin with a Rambo knife.

The Coach was still asleep, then became startled once seeing Country standing beside his bed. Country's punch put the Coach back to sleep.

The Coach re-awakened to Country slapping his face. Then the Coach realized he was butt naked, face down with his wrists and ankles tied to the headboard and foot posts of the bed.

Once Coach gained full consciousness, Country started repeatedly ramming the blade of the Rambo knife up the Coach's ass.

Screams echoed in the dark, but Country kept raping the coach with the knife until the Coach went unconscious and bled out.

Chapter 33
Patience.

I'd taken Candy with me as my assistant into the county jail to help convince Scott and the others to take the deal.

Immediately, Scott's eyes welled up with tears as he hugged his wife. I knew the others would follow Scott's decision.

"Sixty months, but with the drug program, you will be out in three years. Take it or find yourself another lawyer."

"I know you don't think highly of us, but –"

"You're wrong, son. I admire your love for your wife and daughter, and your determination for your talent. What I frown upon is your impatience. I do think this time will help you gain the patience you need and the time to realize what's most important to you."

I did look at him as my son or someone one of my daughters could've been dating if they were alive, they would've been Candy's age.

Candy and I exited the county jail to see a mob of Bible Belt protesters surrounding Preston, who was giving a crate box sermon.

"...This lawlessness was surely a crime of hate. This type of hate has led to the liberation of the church from the government. This type of hate gives a more worldly inclusiveness; this hate waters down and morally weakens the effect of the church's authority!"

Somehow, Preston had gotten wind of the deal the prosecutor was cutting with Scott and the others, so Preston was doing his best to rally as much support as possible to prevent it, be it the media or individuals.

Chapter 34
Chaos.

Country's sense of honor, his dedication to his cause, had him happy, feeling good. He arrived unexpectedly at the hospital where Lulu worked as a nurse. The bouquet of roses he greeted his wife with made the other nurses rush over, gushing over how sweet and romantic Country was.

Country's expression and disposition quickly changed once one of the nurses stopped a handsome young doctor who was passing.

"When are you going to bring me roses?" The doctor and the nurse were noticeably familiar with each other, being flirtatious.

"I'm not your man."

"If you bring me flowers, I'll give you a reason to want to be."

Lulu recognized Country's intense stare and then pulled him away.

"C'mon. Let's go get something to eat."

Country allowed her to guide him, but his eyes were locked on the flirty nurse, and his expression showed his disgust.

"Don't concern yourself with her."

"I don't want you to associate with her anymore."

"Why? She's single, and he's single."

"She's a whore!"

Lulu felt his hand trembling in hers.

"Okay. Okay. Let's just eat before I have to be back."

.....

A full-out onslaught at noon in the projects between gang members and the fake jump-out unit. The bottom-level apartments were trap spots. The gang members had gotten a tip and were somewhat ready when the unit stormed the building. But they weren't prepared for the offensive attack.

Brick and mortar were being eaten away by the high-powered automatic rifles. Bullets were finding their marks through the walls and windows. The blood of the gang members was splattering on the members who weren't hit, but when some tried to break and run, the bullets from members of the fake jump-out unit, covering the exit, ripped through them.

Two gang members jumped out of the window, both blasting their AK-47s with duffel bags on their shoulders, which made the jump-out unit member take cover. The gang members used the opportunity to try to flee.

"They got the money!" echoed over the communication links between the jump-out units.

Three members of the jump-out unit gave chase, running, sprinting through the back of the projects.

The sirens of real police could be heard arriving in the projects, which quickly joined in the chase of the two suspects.

Country was in sniper mode on top of the roof of an apartment building, trying to get a bead on the suspects. He could see the suspects in the laundry room waiting to ambush whoever. But the washers and dryer kept Country from having a clear shot.

"They're in the laundry room." Country's voice blasted over the link, of the other members of the jump out unit.

As Country relayed the whereabouts, he saw that two real policemen were about to stumble into the ambush. Only a fraction of the suspect's head could be seen sticking above the washer. It exploded into a red mist. The other suspect went into shock and stood to have a bullet go through the center of his forehead.

The regular policemen were stunned to realize how close they'd come to being killed.

The other jump-out members quickly arrived and got the duffel bags.

"Secure the perimeter! Wait here until Detective Collins arrives."

The entire jump-out unit entered their vehicles without any hassle.

Ellis Collins arrived and then realized the Birmingham police force had actually assisted the fake jump-out unit. He was pissed!

"All these damn bodies weren't clues that this might be the fake unit!"

"They saved our asses! That's what made me believe they were on our side! You ask me, we should let them clean up the scum." The regular officer was still dumbfounded but appreciative of the fake jump-out unit.

"I don't remember asking!" Ellis Collins really didn't care to hear it.

Ellis Collins went back to the station. He was frustrated, but logged into his PC, checking the different reserve and National Guard armories for break-ins, when the captain summoned him to her office. Agent McWilliams was there beside her.

"Agent McWilliams has a suggestion I think is good. You two divide into two teams to watch the last two known heavy hitters."

"The word on your streets is that they've already hired someone to do our job."

Chapter 35
Surveillance.

Country had parked his truck a block from his house, sitting watching Phil's house.

Once Phil's car passed, Country followed him to a fitness center.

There Country watched through the glass windows of the establishment while Phil worked out with a younger guy who resembled him. Phil vanished toward the back of the building but came back freshly dressed and with a gym bag that he hadn't gone in with. Country then trailed Phil to a nice restaurant where Phil met an attractive woman for lunch -- who afterwards got into Phil's car and served him head, then departed. Phil's next stop was at a barber shop in West End. Country parked in the parking lot with a perfect view of the shop. The barber had been waiting for Phil, so the chair was open.

Halfway through the haircut, the guy from the gym pulled up in a big boy Benz, then somewhat interrupted the barber. Phil seemingly listened, then reclined back in the chair, and the barber continued with the haircut. The Benz pulled off like it was urgent, but Phil's patience made whatever the matter was seem unimportant.

Country was just as patient, and it paid off when Phil pulled into the driveway of an older but huge home in an average-income community. Country knew the neighborhood and circled the block using an alley behind the house.

The Big Benz and about six more luxury cars were in the backyard with heated point men standing post.

Phil only stayed a short time, but Country saw the young guy loading bags into an old model Toyota -- then decided to follow the youngster instead. The guy made stops all over the city, dropping off a bag and receiving bags, while Country was safely out of view but watching.

Country followed the youngster back to the house, arriving after midnight.

The guy and the only guard on post were both bent over unloading the gym bags out of the trunk of the car. Easy prey for Country if he'd wanted, but he wanted Phil.

Chapter 36
Weekend Warriors.

It was Country's weekend to be a weekend warrior, to play sergeant in the Army Reserve. His entire crew was in his unit and had served together on three tours. They'd come home fed up at barely surviving while doing the right thing when seeing people doing wrong and prospering.

Country was the highest ranking out of his crew, but Bo was the one who had come up with the idea of jackin' dope-boys. But the tactical part was all Country.

After roll call, Country and his fake jump-out unit gathered in the back.

"This is the real war we're fighting for our country, for our people, for our community, for the good of America."

The crew laughed at Country's motivational speech, especially Bo.

"We hit the last one on the list. We're done. Chill out. Ellis Collins is asking questions, and the brass is about to do inventory. We've got to think of a way to put this shit back." Bo was truly the only one in the crew that Country respected.

"Phil's still in the game. He's giving orders, moving his shit through Byrd. They're bigger than everybody you had on the list. ..." Money got the others' full attention. "... But Byrd is just his lieutenant."

Country went to lay out his routes of attack, but Bo stepped in,

"I ain't wit it. We're papered up. Let's think of a way to get the shit back before they do an inventory here. Then we'll really have Ellis Collins on our ass."

"We can't put the shit back today. What's one more?"

"I ain't wit it."

Country had trailed Bo since they had left the armory, but once Bo went into the Magic City strip club, Country rode off in another direction.

It was close to midnight. The country was dressed like a homeless bum, pushing his belongings in a shopping cart.

Bo was semi-drunk at an ATM, receiving cash. He turned to go to his car when he was bumped by the shopping cart.

"C'mon, bro! Watch where you're going."

"You're so predictable. ..." Country revealed the 9 millimeter he had aimed at Bo. "... C'mon, bro, we can discuss it in the alley." Then gestured with the gun toward the alley.

"You're gonna kill me so you can keep robbing muthafuckas?"

"We're getting rid of the scum."

"You're sick, you know that, right! You ain't a damn hero. You're a sick killer! That's all!"

Country's emotions got the best of him as he stepped too close to Bo, who knocked the gun out of Country's hand, then hit him with a quick two-piece combination. The punches dazed Country, but Bo's roundhouse kick dropped Country. Then Bo's confidence got the best of him; instead of finishing off Country, Bo allowed him to get up. When Bo attacked again, Country wasn't emotional and saw the punches and used unarmed self-defense to block them.

Country managed to get Bo in a front headlock, then suddenly dropped to the ground with all his weight landing on Bo's neck, instantly breaking it.

Chapter 37
Aftermath.

Bo had been a likeable person at the police station, and a lot of people from his job attended his graveside funeral. Ellis Collins was one, and was surprised to see an entire reserve unit in dress uniform saying good-bye, giving Bo an Army hero's farewell. Normally, only the close friends and family members gathered at the home of the deceased for dinner, drinks, and lies about the good old times but Ellis Collins had gone and managed to get a one-on-one conversation with Bo's wife. She'd noticed how Ellis Collins was studying the pictures; it was somewhat of a shrine of pictures of Bo and his unit posing in different countries.

Ellis Collins actually went to pick up one.

"...When he came back this time, he was different. But in the last six months, he had gotten better. Happier."

"He was always cheerful and polite at the station. I'm so sorry for your loss."

Another woman saw that Bo's wife was becoming emotional and led her away. Ellis Collins then calmly used his cell phone to take pictures of the pictures.

Country had been eyeing Ellis Collins from a distance since the graveyard, but once he saw Ellis Collins questioning Bo's wife, Country quietly went to the members of his crew and whispered a message to each.

They all met back at the gravesite with bottles of liquor.

"He's getting too close." Was the view of the members of the fake jump-out unit.

"We can't kill him. He's a good guy."

Country's moral reasoning had about reached its limits with the crew.

"Fuck Ellis Collins! Who the fuck killed Bo with their bare hands! That's who we need to handle first."

Country kept trying to steer the conversation.

"Word is some D'boys hired a hitter for us. They're afraid of us. We've got 'em scared."

"Look, Country! After this 'last' hit on Byrd, we're laying it down."

"What about the rest of the scum that needs to be cleaned up?"

"This is not Iraq or Afghanistan! We were in this for the money! And no one wants to go to prison! Do you understand?"

Country sized up each of them, then downed the last third of his bottle.

Chapter 38
Pleas.

It was the evening before Scott and the others were to see the judge to enter their guilty pleas and sign the deal with the prosecutor. Their loved ones and friends had pulled them out for a visitation.

Candy and her daughter were on the other side of the glass booth from Scott. Sadie didn't understand why she couldn't hug and sit in her daddy's lap, so she just cried. Candy fought her tears or tried to.

Scott tried to comfort them both.

"It's going to go by fast. I've been writing, plus your CD is blowing up. We're going to be fine."

The more Scott said it, the more he tried to make himself believe it.

"We're still going to miss you. I love you. We love you."

The sheriffs were pressing them, being assholes. They cut Scott and the others' hour visit down to a thirty-minute visit. It was all right with Scott because it was becoming too emotional for him.

"I love both of you more than you'll ever know."

The sheriffs somewhat roughly led Scott out of the room.

Back in the dorm, the mood had changed since Walt B had gotten shipped off to Yazoo. One of the sheriffs had slid a USA Today newspaper to the new shot-caller for the blacks. On the front page was a huge picture of a grand dragon of the KKK and a picture of Big CJ, who was the great-great-grandson of this dead grand dragon.

That night wasn't any request; it was dead quiet. The deputies had separated Scott and the others into different cells.

At breakfast, Scott noticed the whites were suited and booted for war, then realized so were the blacks, sort of a standoff by the stairs to the upper tier. He had just gotten his tray when he spotted two whites and two blacks headed toward CJ's cell. Scott broke toward the stairs to the upper tier with his two homies right behind him. They quickly learned why the whites and blacks were standing by the stairs; Scott and his crew had to fight their way up the stairs.

CJ was brushing his teeth when the hit squad tried to enter his cell. CJ wasn't just big, he was also strong as a mule with a punch like a mule kick. He was handling his own until one of the black guys squeezed rubbing alcohol in his face, then a white guy lit a match and threw it on CJ, setting him on fire.

Screams, agonizing screams, followed.

Scott and the others were willing to give their lives fighting to get to the screams, getting stabbed, but were tossing blacks and whites over the upper-tier rail. As long as Scott and the others stayed close, they were doing fine, but one went after a white boy who had stabbed him. He got him, but before Scott and his homie could get to him, he and two others went over the rail.

Scott made it to the doorway of CJ's cell, then was stabbed in the eye and repeatedly in the back.

The sheriffs finally rushed in once Scott and his crew were down. The other inmates ran to their cells, but Scott crawled to CJ's burning body and lay on him to put out the fire.

Chapter 39
Anguish.

I was in the courtroom, which was packed beyond capacity. They were all waiting for the boys' arrival when the bailiff approached me with the news of the incident. All I could think of was Candy, who was in the row behind me, doing her best to keep Sadie quiet.

I quickly gathered my belongings, then leaned over the rail that divided me from Candy.

"There has been an incident. We have to go to the hospital."

Candy didn't speak. She just grabbed Sadie and their things, then tried to keep up with my pace. I could see she was too afraid to ask what, and I wasn't certain what to tell her.

"Ride with me," was all that came out.

I broke about half a dozen traffic laws getting to the county hospital.

News crews were gathered by the entrance along with several policemen.

"Mr. James, what can you tell us about the attack?"

"You probably have more information than we know."

"Is it true that three of the four are dead?"

Candy became hysterical.

"No-oo! No-oo!"

I consoled her while making our way into the hospital. Ellis Collins was inside and personally escorted us to the ICU floor. I saw the anger in his expression. Once he saw that Candy wasn't looking at him, Ellis Collins gave me a headshake with an expression that let me know it wasn't good.

Ellis Collins took a deep breath, then finally spoke as the elevator doors opened.

"He's pretty bad off, but he's been asking for you two."

Ellis Collins was trying to prepare her, but words weren't possibly adequate. Scott's entire left side of his face was covered with a blood-soaked cloth, and the other side was swollen and black and blue. He was hooked up to every kind of monitor imaginable, but he was fighting to live.

Two doctors were walking away from Scott's bedside as we approached. Candy's tears poured, but she kept her composure. Once she took Scott's hand, he forced his eye open. Candy saw he was trying to speak.

"Don't talk, babe." Her words were forced while she managed to maintain her strength. "Save your strength."

Scott managed to remove the oxygen mask, but sounded exhausted from the effort to breathe.

"I told you I would make your dreams come true even if it killed me. ..."

Candy broke down emotionally, lowering her face close to Scott's, listening to him.

"... I always wanted to be black. Now I am. ..." Instead of being able to laugh, Scott coughed up blood. "... I love you. Live for me." His hand slipped from hers, every monitor sounded, and Candy screamed in anguish along with them.

Chapter 40
Blame and Betrayal.

Ellis Collins needed, wanted, to just stay busy to distract his thoughts from the deaths of Scott and the others. He entered the police station, headed toward his cubicle, and in his line of sight was Agent McWilliams, flirting with the female journalist, Connie Cox. She'd written the grand dragon article, done the research and fact findings.

Instead of Ellis Collins entering his cube, he continued straight for her, then damn near shoved the newspaper in her mouth.

"You did it! You killed them!"

Agent McWilliams and two other detectives pulled Ellis Collins away from Connie Cox, who was in shock.

"Why didn't you write he was married to an African American female and they have a child! And all of them dated black women and denounced any type of racism!" Ellis Collins pushed the Agent off of him. "Get your hands off me! You're just as guilty as her!"

Chapter 41
The Scope of Things.

Country was disguised as a cable repair guy on top of an apartment building. Less than a block below him, he could see his homies standing outside the corner store across from the elementary school. He put his rifle together while contemplating; they were the same guys he'd gone into battle with, celebrated their children's birthdays with, grown up with but his way of thinking was a moral law that superseded all that.

Through the sight of Country's scope, he watched as one of his homies went into the store, another one walked on the side of the store as if to take a piss, while the third was posted, waiting out front, drinking his beer which the bullet from Country's rifle shattered before exploding through the face and out of the back of Country's homies' head.

The noise of the beer bottle drew the one from the side of the building, whose head exploded as soon as he looked around the corner of the building. The last one came out of the store, lighting a cigarette. The bullet exploded the lighter and his head.

Country patiently disassembled his rifle, then climbed off the roof as if he'd finished his repairs. He changed shirts in his truck, then met up with the others at the warehouse. They were all changing into their armored gear.

"Where're little Mike and the rest of them?"

"I don't know. We can do this without them."

Country and his crew had two police patrol units and a Humvee. They drove to the West End area. While the other vehicles drove on, Country parked a block over from the house he'd followed Phil to, then climbed a telegram pole, which gave him a bird's eye view of everything happening inside the house.

There was a plain car patrolling the house, unknown to Country, the driver and passenger were both policemen. Bullets pierced the windshield, striking them in the forehead.

The other members of Country's unit stormed the house, making the people inside retreat to a single room, which Country had a perfect view of through the window. He had the members of his team in his sight, but only put a bullet between Byrd's eyes.

Ellis Collins was at the crime scene of the triple homicide, studying the bodies, the direction they laid, then turned and looked into the distance, focusing on the apartment rooftops.

"Get a team to sweep the rooftops. Did they have identification on them?"

Once receiving the three victims' licenses, Ellis Collins realized they were all members of the reserve unit. He was puzzled, searching for a connection, a reason, when his train of thought was interrupted by a text, which informed him that another robbery had occurred.

Ellis Collins arrived at the second crime scene; the two policemen were dead in the car in front of the house. Again, he looked at the trajectory of the bullets through the windshield, then reversed the path of the bullet from the head of the policemen, through the windshield. He squinted to see the telegram pole.

Inside the home, four bodyguards, two dogs, and Byrd were dead. Ellis Collins left Byrd's body, then went to the window, placing his eye to the bullet hole, and was again able to see the telegram pole.

Later that night, Country and the other three members of his crew met up outside the bowling alley to receive their cut.

"Man, we could really do some–"

"Man, don't start that bullshit! The only thing we're cleaning up is the muthafucka that killed Bo!"

Country manipulated the conversation to its advantage.

"Lil' Mike, Mich, and Sam are dead. Some muthafucka killed them today. I say we snatch a D'boy and make him tell us who they hired."

Chapter 42
Respect.

Ellis Collins interviewed each of the four remaining men on the picture of Bo and the reserve unit; each had a war story for each of their dead comrades, all were heavy drinkers.

"... wasn't anyone better in a jam. We made it through three tours. Shit, you can't imagine. You military?"

"Not anymore. But I was a Marine. I served in Desert Storm."

"So have a drink for fallen soldiers."

Ellis Collins downed his drink and shook off the kick, then somewhat waited for the information to come, which, after two more shots, it did.

"I can't say I hope you catch him. ..." They all were seemingly grieving their loss.

It didn't make sense to Ellis Collins for the reserve team if they were the jackers to be killing each other. So Ellis Collins followed another hunch. He drove out to Coop's ranch.

Coop was rumored to be a hired hitter if the price was right.

Coop was training the pits when Ellis Collins arrived.

"What do you need?"

"It's like that?"

"Yeah. Since Amere's gone, the only time you come out here is when you want something. What is it?"

Coop was right; Ellis Collins had met him through Amere, my brother. Ellis Collins had learned Coop's rep was probably true. But Coop was an honorable man, and he and Ellis Collins had become good friends and highly respected one another.

"I'm sorry about that. I've been busy."

"I know. I read the newspaper."

Coop had super common sense and was fearless.

"You know, word is you were hired to do my job."

"Whoever it is got my M.O. down. I'm looking forward to meeting him someday."

"Thanks, bro. Devin and I are planning a trip to Atlanta to see AJ play. You should come with us."

"We'll see."

Chapter 43
Deletion.

Country was in his home at the computer when Lulu entered their bedroom.

"How much longer before you're done? I need to update my blog."

"I deleted everything so they can't track our electronic footprints."

Lulu was in shock, staring at him as if he'd gone crazy.

"Noooo! Noooo! Are you crazy! My site is bringing in more than both of our paychecks!"

Country had snatched her up so quickly that Lulu didn't know until he'd slammed her against the wall. She was scared, but the only thing she could think of was to kiss him, hug him. She caressed his manhood, and he sexually took out his aggression on her, ripping off her panties, then turning her so she faced the wall while he sexed her. She cried to herself and clawed the wall, but her eyes were on the coke can filled with gasoline.

Country threw her on the bed and continued sexing her, kissing her, whispering to her, "We have to be nonexistent. They know we're trying to save America. I love you. I love you."

Humping harder, faster until she screamed from ecstasy. Both Lulu and Country were exhausted. She tried to roll over, but he kept her in his arms until they both were asleep.

.....

The sun was setting. A bum pushing a shopping cart crossed the street to the parking lot of a bar that the city garbage crew would usually stop at to wind down after work. The three remaining members of Country's crew arrived and were in the parking lot, about to head toward the entrance, when the bum with the shopping cart crossed their path.

"Got some spare change?"

"Hell naw!"

"I heard y'all were looking for me. The person who killed your crew."

Country had caught them by surprise, then started blasting as they tried to run. Country gunned them down, then put one in each of their face, looking at them with disgust on his face.

Country arrived back at his home to find Lulu wasn't there, then went into a fit of rage, tearing the house apart until he broke down in tears. He then composed himself, controlling his feelings.

There was a door that led to the basement of the house, which he'd made into an armory of weapons.

Chapter 44
Discovery.

Ellis Collins had just left the ranch when he received a call to report to the site of another triple homicide.

Agent McWilliams was there supervising the scene when Ellis Collins arrived.

"Are they a part of the unit?"

Ellis Collins accepted the ID and then only nodded. He kneeled and lifted the sheet off a body to see that the face had been blown off.

"Is this your friend's work?"

Ellis Collins still hadn't spoken. He just shook his head.

"How do you know it's not?"

Since McWilliams wouldn't allow Ellis Collins to concentrate, Ellis Collins finally spoke,

"I was with him for the last three hours! This is a sign that these men were a disgrace."

"You're a psychologist now?"

"He thinks he's a hero."

"Do you know who he is?"

"I'm not 100 percent. Go set your trap at your informant's house."

Ellis Collins was heading back to his car while McWilliams continued questioning him from afar.

"Is he the robber or the one killing the robbers?"

"I don't know. Stake out your mark. If he shows, he's both."

Chapter 45
Revelation.

271

Lulu entered the gym somewhat hysterical, interrupting the workshop.

"He's gone out of his mind! He's going to kill me if he finds me!"

Annette's grandmother embraced Lulu, trying to calm her down,

"You're safe now. We're not going to allow anyone to hurt you."

"I had the gasoline. I did like you said, but when I woke up, he was gone. He was gone."

Annette made eye contact with her grandmother, angrily gritting as she took control of Lulu.

"I've got her. Take over the session. No more stories!"

Chapter 46
Retribution.

Country had on his BDU's with two huge duffel bags on his shoulders when he stepped out of his home. He drove by Phil's house to see two men in a plain car sitting on point. He parked a block up the street, then doubled back on foot.

The driver of the parked car outside Phil's home never got to make a sound before Country almost cut off the man's head. In shock, the passenger reached for his gun, but the Rambo knife's nine-inch blade sank deep into his chest.

There was another armed man by the side door to the garage. The Rambo knife went through the back of his neck and came out the front of his throat.

Country held him until he was dead.

The doorbell rang, but when another armed man opened it, he had to catch the dead body of the other guard, allowing Country to simply shoot him in the forehead and walk in over both bodies.

The power in the house went out. Complete darkness. Country placed on his night vision goggles and then walked through the home, shooting everything that moved.

Agent McWilliams and Phil were in the last room in the hall. Country entered the room, which was lit by the street light coming through the bay window. Agent McWilliams quickly identified himself.

"I'm an FBI agent. You don't want to do this."

Phil saw Country was ignoring the agent, still coming in his direction.

"Look, bro, I've got money. Just let me live. I'll give you every cent."

Country raised his gun, but Agent McWilliams stepped in front of Phil, causing Country to pause.

"Why would you want to defend a cancer, a disease infecting our country?"

"You won't kill me," McWilliams was gambling with his own life. "You're a war hero. We're fighting on the same side."

Country fired twice, and both shots ripped through Agent McWilliams' chest.

Phil started crying, covering his face. "Bro, you don't have to–"

Country fired two head shots, making sure Phil was dead.

Chapter 47
Bodies.

Ellis Collins opened the door to Country's home, to find the place a disaster area. He noticed the door that led to the basement was partially open.

With his gun drawn, Ellis Collins crept down the stairs. Once he made sure no one was hiding, Ellis Collins focused on the empty shelves and holders of the arsenal Country had removed. He immediately called Agent McWilliams, but only got a voicemail.

"Shit!"

Ellis Collins ran out to the house to his car while screaming into his cell,

"Officer needs back up at ..."

Three blocks away, Ellis Collins found the patrol unit dead, then the two bodies in the doorway of the house. As he crept through the house, he found more bodies, all trained policemen. In the den, he found Phil with his brains blown out, then shook his head upon seeing Agent McWilliams' body.

Chapter 48
The Battle Within.

Annette and her grandmother were somewhat at odds about Annette taking Lulu to their home.

"You should've taken this child to the police."

"She's terrified of the idea. She thinks he's waiting at any obvious place she should be to kill her. Once she calms down, I'll take her myself. …" Annette's cell rang in a unique tone, and she quickly answered. "Yes, Doctor Wright."

"I can't deal with it. I'm losing it. Things are unraveling."

Annette knew by the commanding tone of the voice that was on the other end. "Breathe, Sergeant Madison. Think reassuring. You have control."

"I don't! This war is controlling me! Making me react! I need to see you!"

"Sergeant Madison, I can schedule you for an emergency session in the morning."

"No! They're closing in on me now! I don't know who to trust! I need to see you now! I need your help. The war is raging!"

"Meet me at my office in an hour."

Annette's grandmother noticed she was putting on her coat.

"Where are you going?"

"I have another emergency to handle. I've given her two Valiums. She should sleep until I'm back."

Ellis Collins stood next to the captain as she addressed the police force.

"We have an all-points bulletin alert out. Pictures of his face and the description of his vehicle have been posted. He is to be regarded as highly armed and dangerous. Yes, this is the same man that many of us have worked with for years. Please do not underestimate him as the mild-mannered janitor. He is a trained marksman and has killed at least eight of our fellow officers. ..."

Ellis Collins' cell vibration drew his attention.

.....

Annette was in her office, watching and listening while Country, in his dress blues, paced the floor.

"I'm defending my country! Why can't they see that?"

"You mean you were defending the country by some of the things you did when you were on tour?"

"That's only the secondary stage. The primary front is here on American soil, against the terrorists among us! But how could they have infiltrated so many layers of my life?

It's bigger than I'd imagined."

Annette could tell his sense of reality was fragile. His suspiciousness.

"What is?"

"The spies! They've infiltrated the police department. My life! How many years have they been planning? How could they have known when I didn't know? They have agents everywhere; I don't know who to trust. They're monitoring me through the cameras in the red lights."

"What are you suggesting?"

"Not a damn thing! I'm telling you, terrorists are in our police force! I had to. I had to!"

He started back pacing, eye suspiciously darting.

276

"You had to what?"

"I had to for the good of our country! They were defending the scum; therefore, they were scum! I had to destroy their cell before it launched its campaign. Their resources make them more powerful than me–"

Annette had realized Country was the killer. But he was observant, careful, because one slip up, he knew he would be caught. His paranoia had him suspicious of everyone, especially Annette, after he realized she was pressing numbers on her cell.

"How can I tell who to trust? Shit, I can't trust anyone! How could they have planted her for so many years?"

"Who?"

"You know who?"

"How do I know, if you haven't told me?"

"Because you are one of them. Her partner!"

She saw him reaching toward her, but couldn't react in time to evade his grasp.

"Take me to your headquarters, and I promise you, you won't suffer."

Country's grip on Annette's arms was strong and tight, so that it scared her.

"This is my only office. I'm your doctor. I'm not a spy."

Country snatched Annette out of her chair and was leading her toward the door.

"Where are we going?" Annette was struggling to remain calm.

"To your home. Now act normal, and no one has to die."

Country released her but poked her with his gun as they stepped out into the hallway, where the security guard was making his rounds.

Country snatched Annette's cell before she could send another text.

Ellis Collins read his text and then interrupted the captain's speech.

"We have his location! He's at the AmSouth Building in Dr. Wright's office."

Ellis Collins called Annette's cell to only get her voicemail, then left the station before the tactical team.

Ellis Collins and several police units sped up the ramp of the parking structure. He saw a glimpse of Annette's car going down the off-ramp.

Once on the parking level of Annette's office, Country's SUV was the only vehicle on the deck.

"You men check her office. You men secure the building. Don't let anyone in or out."

"Where are you going?"

"To follow a hunch."

Four blocks from the building, the traffic of the city schools' basketball tournaments, plus the rain, had the traffic at a standstill. Ellis Collins got out of his car.

He stood on the hood and saw that there was an accident causing the jam.

He then ran past the collision, showing his badge to stop a car that the officers had just allowed to pass.

"Get out!"

"Hell naw! I ain't done nothing!"

"Get out of the damn car!"

"Hell naw! It's storming out there!"

Ellis Collins drew his gun, "Now!"

Once the man got out, Ellis Collins jumped in and drove off, shifting gears, talking to himself.

"Not again!"

Chapter 49
Fight for Survival.

The rain had become heavier as Annette and Country approached the front door of Annette's home. Once the door opened, Country got close to push Annette inside, but she used an unarmed self-defense move with his momentum to flip Country over her shoulder.

Annette's karate kicks caught Country by surprise. But she had to back up from his punches. Once on his feet, he easily blocked her punches and kicks, then threw her across the room into the china cabinet, breaking the glass and dishes.

Annette realized Country was too swift and strong and skilled for her to beat, so she started throwing things at him. He continued to approach until his body went into convulsions as he fell to the floor, then she saw her grandmother standing behind him with her Taser.

Annette immediately started kicking Country.

"Girl, stop! Go get that child so we can get out of here!"

Every time Country moved, Annette's grandmother tased him again. Lulu was still dazed from the medication, so Annette had to support her body weight.

"Let's go!"

Annette's grandmother tased Country one more time before she followed behind Annette and Lulu out into the rain.

It took both Annette and her grandmother to put Lulu into the back seat.

Once they'd gotten into the car, Annette was fumbling with the keys, trying to hurry when the window shattered. It scared them so badly that Annette dropped the keys. Country's arm came through the window, reaching for Annette, who had slid over and was almost in her grandmother's lap.

Lulu awoke to see Country's face peering at her, then immediately started screaming.

Chapter 50
Clash.

Ellis Collins arrived at Annette's house to see Country snatching Lulu through the car window. Ellis Collins drew down on him.

"It's over with Sergeant Madison. Drop the knife."

Country put the knife to Lulu's neck, who was still hysterically screaming.

"All I've done for you! All I've done for my country! This is how you treat a fellow hero!"

Ellis Collins put his gun down while trying to read the context of what Country was saying.

"You're one of them?"

"No. I'm me. But if you kill her, you won't be a hero. You're one of them!"

Country relaxed, thinking about what Ellis Collins had said. He admired Ellis Collins. Annette's grandmother reached out of the window and tazed Country, who fell forward with Lulu, but dropped the knife. Ellis Collins quickly slid Lulu away, but Country recovered before Ellis Collins could get to his gun.

Country tackled Ellis Collins from behind, and both landed hard in the rain and mud.

The gun disappeared in the mud. Hand-to-hand combat: kicks, punches, flips, and slams, but the mud and rain made it hard to keep a grip for a death hold. The car door was jammed; Annette was trying to force it open.

"We have to help!"

Annette's grandmother calmly opened the passenger door. Then both Annette and her grandmother searched the mud for the gun.

Ellis Collins took Country's leg out from under him, slamming him in the mud.

Country spotted the shape of the gun, then started crawling toward it with Ellis Collins on his back.

Ellis Collins managed to get Country in a chokehold. But Country was using all of his strength reaching for the gun while Ellis Collins was using all his strength to apply pressure on the choke hold.

Annette and her grandmother realized what Country was reaching for. His fingers got inches from the gun, then his arm and entire body went limp as he passed out face-first into the puddle of mud.

Ellis Collins released him, then rolled to the gun. He was so exhausted that Annette and her grandmother had to help him to his feet. The rest of the police squad pulled up with sirens blasting.

Ellis Collins, Annette, her grandmother, and Lulu were all shocked to see Country do a push-up out of the mud, then make it to his feet. They stared at him in disbelief.

"Don't move or I'll shoot!"

Country stepped toward them, and Ellis Collins shot him several times in the chest, but the bulletproof armored suit protected him.

"I'm the hero," Country's mind had snapped.

Ellis Collins shot again, and the bullet entered between Country's eyes.

Country stood there for a second. A trickle of blood ran down from the hole, then started to pour. He slowly dropped to his knees and fell forward into the mud.

The other police rushed to the body, but he was dead.

Chapter 51
Inevitably Punished.

It was kind of divine how justice played out, how people were inevitably punished or rewarded for their behavior imminent justice somewhat prevailed.

Pearl and I, along with Ellis Collins and Annette, had gone to the University of Alabama to represent the elementary school from Birmingham that had made it to the state championship, which happened to also be the team of the young Westly girl who was the victim of the sexual assault case. Her mother was there, in loud and alley form, proudly representing her child, who was smiling and having fun on the court, making fantastic shots, incredible passes, and playing terrific defense.

The young girl had the crowd mesmerized her endurance with the drama of her case being so public made us all happy for her.

"It's a wonder how we make it through life."

My statement was just an open thought, but Annette caught my eye, then looked at Pearl's hand in mine.

"We find someone or something to make life worthwhile."

Never the end, just another beginning.